IF YOU LEFT

BOOKS BY ASHLEY PRENTICE NORTON

The Chocolate Money

If You Left

IF YOU LEFT

ASHLEY PRENTICE NORTON

A MARINER ORIGINAL

Mariner Books | Houghton Mifflin Harcourt

BOSTON   NEW YORK   2016

For information about permission to reproduce selections from this book,
write to trade.permissions@hmhco.com or to Permissions,
Houghton Mifflin Harcourt Publishing Company, 3 Park Avenue,
19th Floor, New York, New York 10016.

WWW.HMHCO.COM

Library of Congress Cataloging-in-Publication Data is available.
ISBN 978-0-544-26368-0

Book design by Mark Robinson

PRINTED IN THE UNITED STATES OF AMERICA
DOC 10 9 8 7 6 5 4 3 2 1

With love for my husband, Alex

It is permissible to want.

— DAVID FOSTER WALLACE

IF YOU LEFT

IT MUST HAVE been the first or second week of October by then, or maybe even the third; she didn't know and hadn't really cared. But on that day, time suddenly mattered. Oliver had left only ten minutes earlier to drop Clem at school, but not before kissing Althea on the head and gently pulling the bedroom door closed, thinking she was still asleep. Afterward, he was going to a breakfast meeting at the W Hotel for Spectacle, the company he had started right out of graduate school and that now made millions selling eight-hundred-dollar sunglasses. But Oliver often forgot something and he could easily return to the loft and catch her. She decided to wait another five minutes, which, for her, was an eternity.

Now she was sitting on the floor of their bathroom, knees to her chest, wearing a *Ski Sun Valley!* hoodie and a pair of Oliver's cotton pajama bottoms, the same outfit she had worn for the past three weeks. In her right hand, she held a black croc belt, her Christmas gift to Oliver the year before. She had a hard time imagining herself going into a store — first just browsing, then asking to have something removed from a case, and, finally, going to a counter, digging through her wallet for a credit card, waiting to have the item rung up. It all seemed like so much effort laced with so much optimism.

What she was about to do made a great deal more sense. Fasten the belt around the shower rod, then around her neck. Hop from the lip of the tub. But this would be the fifth time in nine years she had tried, and she had yet to get it right. Always a bridesmaid, never a bride.

She had been flattened by the Tombs since late August. The Tombs weren't the crying kinds of depressions, the ones that came with enough energy and engagement for her to feel sad or hate herself. She didn't have emotions anymore; she had *nothing*. There was just no point. To anything. She couldn't think of anything to do but sleep. She wasn't tired, but somehow, she slept. Until she stopped being able to. Even with the meds Dr. Bair gave her. He tried every possible cocktail, but there was just the bleakness of the Tombs. They said it was *clinical*. It didn't matter what they called it. She just wanted to die. Why didn't she?

But today a radical idea had occurred to her while she was lying in bed, looking at a watch of Oliver's she was wearing. An idea as to why she had survived slicing her wrists to the bone, smashing her car into a tree, overdosing on meds. She wasn't crying out for help or attention. Her manic-depression already gave her plenty of both — she had doctors, meds, hospitalizations — without self-inflicted injuries. She hadn't been playing at suicide. So what was the problem? Now it was obvious. It had been Oliver. Althea had felt like she couldn't do it to him. She'd owed him too much to take her own life.

Oliver had stuck by Althea when she'd been diagnosed as a manic-depressive, fourteen years earlier. He'd been twenty-six, Althea twenty-four, and they'd been married only two years. That time, it had been an episode of the Visions. The upward bounce of the Tombs, where she almost needed sunglasses because everything looked so brilliant and delicious, and gloves because the vibrations she felt when she touched even mundane things like doorknobs or Bic pens were too intense. She wanted to lick them or suck on them, and the golds and blues were sharp enough to slice her eyes. Ollie had thought she was kidding at first, then that she was doing drugs, but when she spent one whole day watching a movie on a loop, repeating the dialogue perfectly after only the second viewing, all the parts, replaying it again and again, for hours, he knew something was wrong and took her to his internist, who sent them to the hospital, immediately.

How many other men his age — *boys*, really — would've stayed by her when they learned there was no cure for her illness, that it would only get worse over time? Probably none. But Oliver had. Why? He'd never told her and she was afraid to ask. She couldn't figure it out. She was like a stock he had invested all of his savings in that had crashed. Why didn't he leave and start over? Love didn't seem like enough of a reason. Could love hold up to this? Maybe it was character. He was the kind of guy to stick it out no matter what. And since he had done that, stuck by her, did she really have the right to choose such a gruesome ending to their marriage? Make him find her covered in bruises and blood or see her stuffed in a drawer at some morgue with bad fluorescent lighting, naked but for a toe tag?

But what if that was actually the right ending for them both? If she were dead, she would no longer be sick; despite what they had told her, she would have found herself a cure. She would be *at rest, God bless*. She knew at first Oliver would feel guilty, think that it was his fault she had died. But then some well-meaning soul would tell him that bipolar people have more success than most populations when it comes to killing themselves, that he really shouldn't take it too personally. And this would signal that enough time had passed for people to say another really stupid thing to him about her — that she was gone but he had to move on. He could now date, even marry, without being the dick who'd left his mentally ill wife. A total win.

She would get it right this time. She would finally have *suicided*. God, she loved how that sounded.

But when she tried to hang herself, the shower rod couldn't sustain her weight and it slid down the wall, taking her with it. *Jesus*. Her sole injury was a laceration from smacking her head on the tub. The only upside of this whole fiasco was that she had found something to do from 8:42 a.m. to 9:06 a.m. Filling time was always a bitch during the Tombs.

Suzanne, Clem's latest nanny, found her trying to clean up the blood on the bathroom floor with a handful of Cottonelle. Suzanne phoned Oliver right away, but the head injury was not bad enough for her to call 911. For the moment, Althea might be sick, but she was safe. Attempting suicide was like having sex: there was always a lull before having another go.

When Oliver arrived, he calmly strode into the bathroom, blazer off, with the composure of someone who could see past a crisis and knew exactly how to fix it.

Oliver gently guided his wife up from the floor and pulled her to his chest; her hair, matted with dried blood, left imprints over his Thomas Pink shirt.

Althea. Oliver never asked Why? or How could you? She could barely talk when she was in the Tombs anyway. Just little whispers that were almost impossible for someone to hear and that she was never quite sure made it out of her head. Oliver took off her *Ski Sun Valley!* hoodie and the Brooks pajama bottoms and threw them in the hamper. She panicked. The shower. Just the thought of it scared her. It made her feel claustrophobic and she didn't even have the energy to put down a bathmat. The two-step process of shampoo/conditioner was overwhelming. Oliver left the room and returned wearing bathing trunks with pink turtles on them.

Oliver slowly led Althea into the shower. He turned the water on, checked to make sure it was comfortably warm, and began gently soaping her back, arms, and breasts with her favorite soap that smelled like lavender. He did her legs, rear, between her legs, stomach. He washed her hair twice, rinsed, and then added conditioner, actually waiting a minute so it would have time to soak in.

When she was at last clean, he shaved her legs, remembering to get her knees, her toes, and around her anklebones. After wrapping her in a white fluffy towel and drying himself, Ollie went back into the bedroom. She knew he was going to pick out some clothes for her to wear to the hospital and then pack for her, like he always did. She took a few breaths before heading in behind him. Even with Oliver's help, the whole process seemed overwhelming.

They always used the same bag for the hospital. It was a purple canvas T. Anthony duffle with her initials on it, AJW. Purple was her favorite color. Oliver always had a purple hue in every Spectacle line just for her. She watched as Oliver packed the purple bag. She had managed somehow (had Suzanne helped her?) to get the clothes on but not to brush her teeth or her hair or put on deodorant. The elastic waist of the skirt dug into her skin, and the T-shirt was just a little too tight. She was dying to go into the hamper and pull out the *Ski Sun Valley!* hoodie, but she couldn't take everything off again.

All the clothes Oliver packed were baggy and soft. Someone might have thought she had a special wardrobe just for her inpatient stays, but Althea dressed this way in her normal life too. She liked flowy skirts in fabrics like velvet or cashmere or crushed silk; she hoped they made people think she was ethereal, sensual, spiritual. Of course, she was none of these. She was dark, intense, and creatively brilliant. Like her photographs. She did work between breakdowns. Had had a few shows, gotten a few reviews, sold a few things. Successful by art-world standards. She didn't make a lot of money doing it, but she told herself that wasn't the point. Being a photographer made her feel like a grownup. More important, it served as evidence that she wasn't always ill.

Oliver didn't really approve; he thought she should be doing something more soothing. He worried her work might be a trigger. After all, her themes tended toward sexuality. Fertility. Fantasy viewed through poststructuralist, feminist, or whatever other academic theory had inspired her that period. Most people couldn't see past the naked bodies and thought her work was just pornographic, obscene. But Althea didn't care.

Oliver went into the bathroom and Althea watched him as he packed the toiletries. A purple toothbrush and travel-size Crest. Travel-size Finesse shampoo and conditioner. Brush. Deodorant. Soap and lemon body scrub. They were all new. Kept under the sink. He said that it was good to have backups for those kinds of things because you never knew, but she did know. It was for trips like these.

Ollie stopped packing her clothes and she thought of what

he hadn't put in, the contraband he knew not to take. No headphones. (She could hang herself, they said. Really? How would that work? The belt hadn't.) No computers. (She wasn't sure why. To keep you from Googling obscure ways to hurt yourself?) No meds. (They had them there. They were like a hotel with stocked minibars.) But Oliver knew all the rules by now. They were straightforward and immutable, like getting through the TSA. But New York–Presbyterian wasn't hunting down terrorists, protecting the homeland from stealth attacks. They knew she was the enemy, and the target was herself.

So Oliver packed two down pillows. A cashmere throw. Quilted slippers. When he finished, he zipped the duffle and checked for the luggage tag, like the bag might actually get lost on some airport carousel, like she really was flying somewhere, maybe going to Canyon Ranch for ten days. He organized the change on his dresser by denomination while watching CNBC, then took the dry cleaner's plastic off his shirts, which both soothed and unsettled her. She had tried to hang herself a few hours ago, but Oliver was unruffled. She was sure he would go back to work after she was situated, then go for a run when he got home, maybe meet friends for drinks later. Life went on.

Finally, it was time. As she followed Oliver out of the bedroom, she saw her olive army rucksack that held her Canon, wallet, keys, iPhone, and iPad sitting on the chair by her bed. The bag she took everywhere, even to some of the cocktail parties Oliver dragged her to. She hadn't carried it for months. Of course not. Its hibernation had foreshadowed the appearance of the fucking purple duffle.

They walked into the living room. Suzanne was standing

by the door wearing jeans and a teal wool sweater that had pilled. Althea could tell that the girl was struggling. Oliver had warned her when she took the job that this might happen, and Suzanne had nodded, *No problem*, but now it seemed she was thinking it kinda was.

Ollie went over and put his hand on Suzanne's shoulder, squeezed it, then smiled at her. Ollie said something, but Althea was too agitated to hear what it was. She was desperate now to get to the elevator, didn't want to have to touch Suzanne, didn't want to talk to her about Clem, to try to seem concerned about how her daughter would get through the next ten (or more) days without her. But Ollie read Althea's *I need to go now* look, opened the door to the foyer, and gently walked her out. She put her head on his shoulder as they rode down to the first floor, and for the first time in what must have been an eternity, Althea felt something close to relief.

ONCE THEY WERE on their way to the hospital, she became increasingly desperate to get there. Even though Oliver patted her hand and smoothed her wet hair over her shoulders, she compulsively bit her lips and rocked back and forth, and when they got stuck behind a garbage truck, she almost got out of the taxi and screamed.

When they finally arrived at the hospital, the nurses said her doctor had called to say she was being admitted but her bed wouldn't be ready for an hour. They went to the Au Bon Pain in the atrium to kill time. Oliver bought her a sticky bun and a large coffee. She hadn't had coffee since August. It was too much of a project, all that stirring of the sugar and milk, then the blowing and slow sipping so it didn't burn your tongue. Finishing it would take forever. But any coffee she got on the Unit would be cold (so people couldn't burn themselves or others, she supposed) and watery (to keep the patients from, God forbid, getting some kind of caffeine buzz), so she decided to give it a try.

She started to rip open an Equal but her hands shook so bad from the lithium that she ended up spilling the white powder all over the table. Oliver smiled at her indulgently like she was Clem (although Clem was fastidious when she ate), but she felt humiliated and decided to give up on the coffee and go for the roll instead. She picked some nuts off the top and put them in her mouth, but her throat was so dry she couldn't swallow and almost choked. She spat the nuts out onto the waxed paper and watched Oliver drink his lemonade and eat a cranberry scone.

Finally, Oliver checked his watch and noted the hour was up, and they went back to the Unit.

A nurse wearing teddy bear scrubs buzzed them in and immediately ransacked the purple duffle and frisked Althea. Teddy Bear Scrubs found only one thing that wasn't allowed on the Unit and would have to be sent home with Oliver: Althea's channel-set diamond wedding band. It was expensive and could get stolen by one of the other patients. But her hands were so puffy now that the ring was embedded in her finger. As much as she tugged at it, it would not come off. Teddy Bear Scrubs gave her Vaseline to rub over it and then yanked at it herself, but it still wouldn't go past her knuckle. Althea was afraid Teddy Bear Scrubs would get some tool from the nurses' station and cut it off, but she must have been feeling generous (or exhausted; who knows how many admits she had had that day), and she said she would make an exception just this once and let Althea keep the ring, but if anything happened, she'd hafta take responsibility.

When Teddy Bear Scrubs nodded to the door, signaling that it was time for Oliver to go, Althea was beside herself. She started to sob. It was the first time she had cried in months. Ollie handed her his blue-and-green-checked pocket square, but she was too upset to unfold it and bring it to her face. She grabbed the lapels of his blazer, held on to him like it was the first day of kindergarten and she was one of the clingy kids. He felt so solid, so reassuring, like nothing could take him down, not even this, not even this time. He held back from a full hug, like he didn't want to give her the false hope that he was going to stay after all. But he had to stay. Couldn't she get five more minutes? But for what? What could she do in that time?

But Oliver was not *possibly* leaving, he was *definitely* leaving her, now. His departure had nothing to do with her (husbands, like everyone else, were allowed only during visiting hours), so there was nothing she could do to make him stay. He pried her hands from his blazer and patiently explained that he needed to tell Clem what had happened (and she did her best to act like *Of course you do*), get some work done, and otherwise *handle* things. But Oliver promised he would be back for the evening vids, just like he always was.

But his coming back missed the point. She knew, from all the times she had been on the *inside*, that after the door closed, she became the patient and he the visitor. They were married, man and wife, but now, once again, here was that fucking door. The one that only people in scrubs with ridiculous patterns could open. The one that she had to *earn the privilege* to go out of for ten minutes at a time, accompanied by someone who'd most likely be wearing clogs, maybe to the parking lot, maybe even to the atrium, just so she'd have something else to do besides pace the hall. The door came between Ollie and her like a divorce. What about *What God has joined, let no man put asunder?*

But what if one day, Oliver just didn't come back for her? What if that door became too much of a hassle; what if he just got sick of waiting for the buzzer? She never outright begged him to promise he would always, always come. Even in that state, she knew begging would make her seem desperate, and she was too desperate to seem desperate. She hoped Oliver would think she was just vulnerable. Vulnerable wasn't repulsive; vulnerable drew one in, made one feel protective. He couldn't abandon vulnerable. But Althea never completely trusted this logic, or trusted him. Didn't a person get only so many chances? Vulnerable or no? So even though he said, *See you tonight, Althea,* after the door closed (and locked), Althea kept crying, harder than she had ever seen Clem do, long after Oliver could have heard her.

The stay that October was the same and different than all the others. There were the same assortment of patients: some manic, some depressed, all annoying the shit out of one another. The nailed-down TV, stuck on one channel, that she didn't even have enough concentration to watch. There were the visits from psychotherapists and social workers, all of them asking the same questions about her history, asking how she was feeling now. There were the meds, the meds the patients had to wait in line for several times a day like they were buying tickets for the cinema, and when they got to the window they were handed fistfuls of chalky pills in paper cups, institutional origami. There were the endless "checks": someone coming into their rooms every fifteen minutes all night long to make sure they weren't engaging in any self-harming behavior.

As Althea saw it, the whole program, despite the pretense of busyness, was really just a way of waiting out a relapse. As if, if they took away all her freedom and made things tedious enough, she would (like a child in an extended time-out) just snap out of it. But seven days into her stay, she wasn't any better. She didn't cheek her meds. Didn't pick fights with the nurses. (Rebellion was apparently a sign of recovery.) She was one of the tough cases. There was one thing that they hadn't tried yet, one thing that was often effective although they didn't really know how it worked. It was kind of like rebooting a computer when you had a glitch, they said. Sometimes, that simple action did the trick.

But she soon learned that electroconvulsive therapy was nothing like rebooting a computer. It was at least one hundred times worse than anything she had ever done to herself.

At the beginning of each *treatment*, as they called it — like it was a facial or something — she lay on a gurney as an anesthesiologist mashed a plastic mask over her nose and mouth and told her to count backward from one hundred. Althea started counting and tried to let her mind wander and think about everything else but that mask. The feeling of the cold spots on her temples, where they had smeared clear gel, stuck the metal disks that attached by tiny cords to the box with knobs on it. The woman with a severe bun wearing a brown tweed suit who stood behind her head, the one who turned the knobs, administered the shocks, who fried her brain. Althea couldn't see her. What was the woman's expression? Focused? Impatient? Bored?

But it didn't work. She couldn't escape the mask. Althea would get to ninety, eighty-eight, eighty-six, and she still wouldn't be under. It felt like her lungs were filling with sand, like she was going to suffocate. Althea couldn't breathe, she really couldn't. She thought she was going to die. She would finally lose consciousness somewhere around eighty-four, but *Jesus*, an eternity. After seventeen brutal *treatments*, she was considered well enough to be discharged.

SHE AND OLIVER had met at NYU. She was nineteen; he twenty-one. They were both from the West Coast — Oliver, San Francisco; Althea, Los Angeles. Oliver was WASP handsome: light brown hair, green eyes, straight nose. He wasn't particularly tall (five eleven) or exceptionally athletic (he played tennis and squash but always preferred the gentleman's game to running down points, even at that age), but his extreme confidence bumped him up from handsome to gorgeous. She was beautiful in a quirky way, one that not all men understood. She had brown eyes that were a little too big for her face, wavy dark hair down her back, and a prominent nose. She did a lot of yoga because it seemed alternative, which she liked, but she ultimately hated it because all the time she was forced to spend in her head meditating stressed her out. She wore makeup rarely but boots and floppy suede hats always, even in the summer.

She was medium-boned but small-breasted, which made her self-conscious, even though she'd had four boyfriends by the time she met Oliver, two of whom had proclaimed *I love you*, and so far she'd had a terrific sex life.

After three weeks of dating, they still hadn't slept together. They'd made out so intensely they had both shuddered; Althea had let him pull back her underwear and ease his fingers inside her, and she had even given him a blowjob, swallowing as he came (most of the girls he knew spat it out in the sink). But Althea could tell that, as *excellent* as these things might have been (that was one of his favorite words, *excellent*), Ollie was getting impatient. Why hadn't they gotten to the end zone? What was the fucking problem?

The fact was, she was afraid. Ollie wasn't like all the other boys she had dated; there was something about him. He was solid. More mature than the boys she knew. It had been only three weeks but she adored him. She knew most people would say that for her to *adore* Oliver at this point was absurd. But she didn't care. She wasn't making it up. She had amazing intuition. *She just knew*. She couldn't mess this up. She had to have him.

She wanted their relationship to stay in the beginning stages for as long as possible. In the waiting part. People rarely walked away during the waiting part. Because once you had sex, it was anybody's guess what would happen. The guy could be a dick and move on, or he could decide to stay. The key was timing. If she made him wait too long, Oliver would give up, find some-one else. But at least he wouldn't have dumped her. Not really.

One night, sitting in his room, she waited for him to kiss her. And he didn't. Then she waited for him to ask her to leave. But he didn't. Instead:

Althea, what is it? I mean, are you a virgin or something?

She looked at her boots. Touched her hair. Her whole plan suddenly seemed stupid and immature.

No.

So what's the deal?

There's no deal.

Then why won't you sleep with me?

You never asked.

Althea, come on . . .

I guess I just wasn't ready.

Why?

Doesn't matter.

Are you now?

Was she? Yes, she guessed she was. Yes. But she still didn't want to risk an in-out-goodbye. Even if he did dump her in the end, she wanted him to remember her.

Ollie. What if I asked you what gets you off? I mean really *gets you off . . .* Had she actually said that? And what if he couldn't think of anything?

But she knew everyone had something. Something the mind keeps in reserve to make sure the body can always make the transition, get to the go mark. Hers was parallel parking. It grew out of one night she'd spent with a boyfriend back home. It was two a.m. and she was sitting on a windowsill in his house in Brentwood. They had just had sex so she was in that opened-up, vulnerable state when little things make an impression. He went to move his car and the way he slid it, effortlessly, between two others, no big deal, triggered something in her, made her go completely wet. And every time Althea thought about parallel parking, she was completely wrecked. She wanted to know what did it for Oliver.

He hesitated just long enough to make her regret asking.

But then he said, *Could you maybe touch yourself while I watch?*

At first, instead of *while I watch*, Althea heard *on my watch*, like he would be setting an alarm, clocking her progress. Althea could count the number of times she had masturbated in her life and it had always underwhelmed her. She thought the rubbing was pleasant (she got to control the pace and knew exactly where it felt best) and soothing (it calmed her mind, stopped the thinking, the constant thinking, and made her sleepy), but her hand got tired after about five minutes and she always gave up before orgasm. She came easily with the boys she dated (Gordon, a surfer she had been with, called her his Hawaii 5-0), so she didn't need to *order in*, as she referred to masturbation. But here she was in kind of a hybrid situation. He was asking her to take matters into her own hands so he could — what, supervise?

The more she thought about it, the more complicated Oliver's request seemed. She didn't want to mess up. Should she keep her eyes open or closed? Should she look at him or pretend he wasn't there? What was she supposed to think about? Was she supposed to tell him what she was thinking or make something up? What if she couldn't come? Should she fake it? She never had. It was one of the things she swore she would never do, but she couldn't really sit there touching herself for hours and not come, could she? The whole thing was just too much. But he was standing there waiting for her to start.

She started touching — rubbing? stroking? — herself. Then she glanced up and saw Oliver watching her. He looked absolutely dazed. Awed. Grateful. On the verge of tears. She realized that this was the first time a girl had done this for him. She wanted to reach up and pull him down to her. Take off his clothes. Touch his back, kiss him. But she knew it would ruin it. So she kept going. She started to make noises (for real) and she thought she had gone too far and maybe he thought she was just being cheesy. She made herself look at him again (he still wasn't touching himself, was just standing, fully clothed, at the end of the bed, watching her) and she saw it: they were both waiting for something, something they would die if they didn't get — or maybe they would die if they did — but it wasn't an orgasm. When the orgasm came (for either one of them), it would erase all this, spoil everything. But the end did come, it had to. It was all too intense, and they'd never felt as close to each other again as they had right before they came (he first, then her), and then it was all over. Oliver fell into the bed and she buried her face in the comforter and tried to steady her breath.

They did have a round two that night, and it was pleasant, like meeting an old friend for a glass of wine. They knew each other intimately now, but there was a kind of sadness to it since it was not the first time. And then it slipped out: Oliver told her he loved her. She wasn't expecting this. She couldn't say it back, not yet; she had to let him own it, not let it get lost in reciprocity. But even though she was planning to make him wait (just a little bit), she knew it was decided. They would be together forever.

And so they got married right after she graduated. At twenty-two, she was the giddy child bride, and Oliver, at twenty-four, the guy who had jumped the line, found the right girl, and gotten to the real part of life while most other boys his age were still throwing up at kegs and bringing home women they hated themselves for in the morning. Just wasting time. But Althea and Oliver lived in a three-bedroom prewar on lower Fifth. She was taking graduate courses in photography, still at NYU; he was getting his MBA at Columbia. He already knew he was going to start his own business.

They were completely wrapped up in each other. They didn't deal with their families like most married couples; they didn't negotiate, divvy up who and where for Thanksgiving, Christmas, or even Easter. It wasn't that they were too busy, too far away (they could certainly afford airfare to the West Coast), or wanted to start their own traditions. No — Oliver's mother was an alcoholic, Althea's mother was a depressive, and Althea's sister was a bitch. They both swore these situations weren't tragic, merely annoying, but they were reason enough for them to have just each other. But soon after, of course, it was the three of them: Oliver, her, and her disease. And even though Ollie was accepting of the situation, said there was always some kind of problem that revealed itself only once the rings were on, she still thought it totally sucked that she had to be the one who'd had the bomb planted in her luggage and who'd unknowingly rolled it across their threshold.

Oliver eventually came up with a master plan to *manage* her illness. She thought of it as the Great Trifecta.

Part one: Seeing Dr. Bair, a psychopharm, three times a week. Even when she was well. (No problem. He was nice enough. His couches were comfortable and he didn't expect her to talk about her childhood.)

Part two: Taking her meds. A potent cocktail of five — lithium, Celexa, Abilify, Lamictal, and Seroquel. (Small problem. Althea wasn't stupid enough to go rogue and not take them, which would hasten a relapse, but the side effects . . . the side effects were just horrible. The worst: the weight gain and loss of sex drive. Well, no; she was still interested in sleeping with Oliver, could get going if she really put her mind to it, but the meds caused a complete inability to orgasm. No matter how Althea tried, she just couldn't come. Dr. Bair said it would get better. Her body would acclimate. Or, if not, he would replace the meds with different ones that wouldn't cause this *snafu* — as he put it — as soon as he was sure she was absolutely stable. Because, Dr. Bair said, she was just too young to give that up.)

Part three: Adopting Clem. (She saw no upside to part three. Didn't see how it would help her recover; in fact, she didn't see how it wouldn't force a relapse. But she knew Oliver didn't view it that way. He considered it his ace in the hole.)

Five years after her first episode, when Althea was twenty-nine, Ollie announced that he wanted a family. Or, rather, a family that was bigger than the two of them. And since she had to take all of those get-well-soon pills — which would have been like maggots to any fetus she conceived, possibly eating away at its face, brain, and limbs — Oliver told her they would adopt. And though she hadn't wanted kids even before she got ill — she just didn't relate to them; at her worst, they annoyed her — she knew that, after all she had put him through, she owed him.

So along came Clem, a baby made and carried by a sixteen-year-old girl from Indiana, a baby who was blond and blue-eyed to Althea's brown hair and brown eyes. Who smelled like . . . nothing. Or that nasty formula she kept spitting up. Who was mostly bald so there was no hair to play with. Who screamed so loudly, Althea could hear her through her noise-canceling headphones. She tried giving her a bath one night, thinking that might be some kind of bonding experience, but the corpulent baby nurse they had hired to live in for Clem's first year snatched Clem away from Althea and shoved her out of the bathroom, saying she should always run the water first before getting the baby undressed.

She had named her Clementine because she thought it sounded cool: unique and British. She bought lots of things — diaper bags, onesies, T-shirts — and had Clem's name printed on them in hip colors like olive green and brown, hoping it would make her like Clem better, but at the end of the day, Clem was still a baby she didn't like dressed in clothes she'd bought in SoHo or Brooklyn. Althea wanted to talk to Oliver about how she felt, but it was the kind of thing you had to dance around and only hint at until you were certain the other person felt the same way (like being in love). But Oliver gave no sign of being anything other than completely besotted. He had a tiny pair of orange (clementine) sunglasses made for Clem, took her out in that horrible Swedish baby carrier. (What was wrong with the Bugaboo stroller they'd spent seven hundred dollars on? Why did he have to strap her on like he was some kind of primate?) They even took Clem out to dinner with them to places like Balthazar and Mercer Kitchen; Oliver used to be outraged when people showed up there with kids, but now he found it endearing when Clem screamed or repeatedly threw food out of her high chair.

So there would be no big admission on Althea's part, no conspiring with Ollie about how this thing just wasn't quite working out the way she'd expected. If Althea had said so much as *I'm kind of having a hard time here, I thought I'd like it more,* Oliver would have known that the *it* she was referring to was not motherhood but Clem. And he would have said, *Well, get over it, Althea. Get over it, or get out.* (This was what she thought, anyway.) And for a minute, she would have not only disliked Clem but actually hated her.

WHEN ALTHEA WAS released from the hospital this time, she wasn't exactly sick, but she wasn't exactly well. She facetiously said she was *just swell* when asked. She would have to go back to the hospital for after-care outpatient treatment that would supposedly give her the *life skills* to function like a normal person.

After-care went on for six interminable weeks. She found most of it totally useless, but because of her willingness to par-

ticipate, her doctors decided it was safe to take her off Seroquel. The med had made her unable to get up before ten a.m.
or stay up past nine unless she drank so much coffee and Diet
Coke her hands shook and she had terrible diarrhea. When Althea was on it, her thoughts were slightly foggy (enough that
she couldn't remember names or past conversations) and her
speech was a bit slurred (she had once been pulled over for
a suspected DWI and was let go only when she blew a zero).
On the Seroquel, she was always twenty to thirty pounds over
her ideal weight (read: she had to ask if they had dresses above
size 12 when she was shopping, and in SoHo, they usually
didn't).

The premise behind the after-care program seemed like
complete bullshit to her. Hadn't her doctors told her over and
over that what she had was a chemical imbalance — i.e., something she was born with? Now along comes after-care, offering
cognitive solutions, *tools for her toolbox*. But she figured she
didn't have the luxury of debate. Even though the whole thing
was probably a ploy for the doctors to keep an eye on her just a
little longer or to provide some structure for her day, she knew
she needed to stay for Oliver. Reassure him that she really was
getting well this time. So she went to group discussions about
managing depression and anxiety that were run by an ebullient man, Stuart, who had most definitely never experienced
either. He raised the pitch of his voice a few octaves whenever he addressed the group's members (whom Althea came
to think of as the *recoverings*), as if they were children, which
completely pissed her off, so she made a point of tripping over
him whenever she entered or left the room. Stuart wore a suit

and a Ferragamo tie, and Althea was sure he was one of those men (and they were always men) who'd decided to quit their hedge-fund jobs and try to make a difference (and who were now probably rethinking that decision).

She also did dialectical behavior therapy, designed for people who had fallen off the ladder of life and into hard times, which seemed to describe all the recoverings passing their days at the center, some still peeing in cups to be tested for substances. DBT was all about self-soothing, self-love, and radical acceptance of one's situation. She was supposed to make lists of things that she thought were relaxing, but the only thing that really did the trick for her was sleep. So she got creative and wrote *sucking on Popsicles, tying sailing knots, doing origami* (all lies, of course, but she wasn't going to put down *taking baths, petting cats,* and *knitting* like almost every woman there did).

And then there was radical acceptance, a major tenet of DBT. Radical acceptance went something like this: *Accept that you will never recover completely. That you will probably be in this same seat in two years. That you are indifferent (on a good day) to your kid.*

Wow, helpful, she thought.

For the first time in DBT, Althea asked a question.

So, basically, if you're screwed, you're screwed? The concrete has dried and we should just suck it up?

No, said Tammi, the DBT therapist, *you're forgetting the* now. *Accept the now and it's less painful. You just have to wait it out. Then comes the future. Who knows what's going to happen in the future.*

Oh.

Althea had never thought she had control over her now. When she was sick or uncomfortable, she just did everything she could to make it go away. But still, she hoped another big sucky now wasn't about to come along for her to deal with, accept. She was sure it would fell her.

SHE NEVER TALKED to Oliver about what went on in after-care or, really, what happened when she was in the hospital, and he never asked. Why rehash all the drama? They had survived once again. Or maybe the lack of discussion was just WASP reticence. She often wanted to tell him how sorry she was, how bad she felt about everything she had put him through, and the imaginary conversation always went something like this:

Ollie, I know it's all been horrible. The past fourteen years. And now the treatments . . . I'm so sorry. Really.

And then Ollie would answer, *No worries. It's fine.*

So we're good?

We're good.

I'm going down to get some macaroons.

Can you bring me up some water?

BUT SHE KNEW if things were going to work out in the long run, if she wanted to keep Oliver from getting so sick of her one day that he left without even a note, she needed to do something to show she had changed. Not reaching some small personal goal, like learning to make coq au vin or running a marathon, but a big-picture thing, something that would convince Oliver she was finally getting her shit together. Of course she knew what this something was. Even if they didn't have soul-baring conversations, Althea knew him better than anyone.

What mattered to him was not reclaiming their prior sex life, which maybe, with her now off the Seroquel, they just might, nor was it her being more social, more engaging, more fun. It wasn't even her doing a better job managing her manic-depression: eating healthier, getting more exercise, et cetera. Not that he wouldn't appreciate these things, but she knew he had learned to make do without them, had even given up on them.

But there was one thing that Oliver was still waiting for her to do. After all these years, he was still holding out, still giving her chances. He wanted her to *show up* for Clem. *No, not show up. That's what nannies do, Althea.* He wanted her to be Clem's mother. *Care about her. More than care, Althea. Mothers do more than care.* Oliver wanted her to *love* Clem. Yes, that was it. Oliver wanted her to love Clem.

But how could she? Could she really make herself love someone? She hadn't loved anyone but Oliver since they'd met. If somehow she did manage to love Clem, would she love Oliver less? Would he resent her for that? Hate her? Because as far as she could tell, once she'd gotten sick, that was really all she had to offer him: total devotion. But maybe that wasn't enough anymore. Maybe he was closer than she'd thought to getting on the road to being done with her once and for all.

OLIVER WAS IN a mood the days following her completion of after-care. He was sarcastic, edgy, dark. He was always like this whenever she finished treatment, as if all the decency in him had been depleted when she was sick. She tried to make it up to him, initiating cheery conversation, complimenting the gains he had made at the gym (yes, she swore she could tell), and, when all else failed, giving him his space, but no matter what she did, he still remained just this side of mean. She told herself it wasn't her, as she always did; maybe Ollie was stressed because sales were down at Spectacle; who bought eight-hundred-dollar sunglasses in December? But of course, plenty of people did — Christmas was coming up, and everyone was off to warm destinations for the holidays. And no matter what month she got well, Oliver always acted like this. So she hid out in her office and cried.

But one night, she didn't have that luxury. They had a Christmas party to go to. She hated parties. She found them excruciating. And not because, in the past, her knees had been so swollen she couldn't cross her legs. Or because she always asked the same questions twice because she wasn't paying attention. Or because she had to fold her arms across her chest so no one could see her hands shake. No, these things were downright enjoyable compared to what Oliver always did to her. Every time she could walk again, it seemed, he took her out to a party and made her fall.

He had several favorite party *gotchas*, as Althea thought of them. That night in December, after already being a total shit at home, he opted for one of the classics. He went to the bar to get them drinks and returned with a pretty girl in tow, no wrinkles on her face or forehead, which Althea knew was a gift of youth and not Botox. She had perfectly streaked hair that she probably maxed out her one credit card to maintain. Althea had barely taken her first sip of Diet Coke when Oliver whipped out his iPhone and asked the girl if he had punched in her number correctly. The girl (Paula?) blushed and stammered that she hadn't given it to him. (Jesus Christ, why was he doing this? The girl was clearly freaking out. Was she going to get in trouble? Oliver would text her later in the week and ask if she was *up for a fuck*. Althea had seen one of his texts. He didn't waste time with the *how r u*'s that boys used.) But the cheating bothered her less than the public humiliation of having her husband parade another woman right in front of her. Maybe it wasn't that awesome to think about Oliver going down on a twenty-five-year-old girl, her coming about two minutes after he pushed his fingers inside her while she was still dressed and then coming again as he went down on her and then coming again when he put her ankles up by her ears and . . . but at least Althea wouldn't have to stand there and watch.

But as for Ollie's asking for the girl's number right now, what were Althea's options? Glare at Paula until she went away? Laugh like a good sport? Or throw a drink in his face? Isn't that what most wives would do? But did she really get all of the privileges and rights thereof anymore? So she excused herself to the bathroom and hung out there and, later, in the foyer until Oliver came to get her. As bad as it was, she went home with him, and they would never discuss it.

She spent the day after that party in bed recovering. If she didn't drink enough water on the meds, she got terrible migraines. When she finally got up, it was almost six p.m. Althea wanted to spend the rest of the evening in her room watching movies on her computer and eating the stash of Milk Duds she kept in her bedside table, but she knew she had to at least try to start bonding with Clem. Otherwise she might lose her resolve.

Althea was actually afraid of the girl. She was not easy. Not difficult, per se, but intense, and unusual. Clem was a ridiculously intelligent nine-year-old; she used words like *conundrum* and *atavistic*. She read books that challenged Althea. She was prone to irony and sarcasm but never swore. She liked to silk-screen T-shirts, loved to ride horses, and she collected maps: road, subway, museum — really, all maps. She was obsessed with directions. But Althea just didn't know how to interact with her. How to find common ground. She could have just sat and watched her, listened to her, but she didn't even know how to do that.

She got dressed in jeans and one of her MOMA T-shirts, then walked downstairs into the kitchen. Suzanne and Clem were eating rice and lentils in majolica bowls passed down from Oliver's mother and drinking green tea from majolica mugs. Clem loved green tea.

What's on the menu this evening? Did Althea really say this every night? For the first time, she realized how absolutely ridiculous this was.

Hey, Lune.

That was what Clem called her. It wasn't one of those cute things that she'd come up with when she was a toddler. It was Althea who'd made it up, baptized herself for Clem. When Oliver asked her why, Althea said that Lune was special; it was steady, a bright guardian light. But really, Althea had no idea why she'd chosen it. Because after purple, her favorite color was silver? Because the only children's book she could name offhand was *Goodnight Moon*? Because (of course not really, but still) it was the first half of *lunatic*?

Whatever the reason, Lune still sounded better than Mommy. Mommy was a mess. You traded in your ID badge and came out with this. You weren't unique anymore; you were part of a tribe. You had the same name as every other woman at the playground: *Mommy, Mommy, Mommy*. You weren't a stay-at-home *woman*; you were a stay-at-home *mom*. You referred to the women you met as your mommy friends, and you even referred to yourself that way: *Mommy loves you*. Althea wanted no part of it. Up in the sky. Shiny, bright, untouchable.

But now here she was, in the kitchen with Clem and Suzanne. Althea wasn't quite sure what to say so she repeated her question, like she was on the spectrum (as people now termed it) or, at best, socially challenged.

What's on the menu this evening?

Lentils and rice. Want some, Lune? Clem said. But Althea hated lentils. They made her think of something you would scrape off the bottom of your shoe after walking on a muddy trail. And rice — Oliver always tried to feed her rice mixed with applesauce when she was in the Tombs, like she was an infant. But thank God, they were almost finished eating anyway. The food was probably cold. Althea figured it was fair to decline. She would try this another night. Come after they were done.

No, thanks.

But then she saw Clem looking at her. She had her elbows on the table, her chin in her hands, and she smiled slightly. Althea knew that look. Clem did it every time Althea acted like, well, herself and withdrew from Clem. She would have thought it was a kind of sophisticated form of crying, efficient in that only she understood it, except that even she knew that there was nothing sophisticated about having your feelings hurt. But she was surprised (hopeful?) that she still had some kind of effect on Clem. She'd thought the girl would have given up long ago.

So she stayed. And said:

I will have some tea, though.

Clem and Suzanne stared at her. There was an awkward pause and Althea realized that, despite Clem's offer, they really hadn't expected her to stay and had no idea how to work her into their evening. And she didn't know how to be worked in. What would they talk about? Althea's stay at New York–Pres? How Suzanne's snow-globe collection was coming along? Clem's . . . Jesus, she really didn't have a clue what the girl was into these days. And it wasn't like she could ask. That would make her look as clueless as she was. But she tried to reassure herself she still had a right to be there; she and Oliver had used her money to buy the loft. She had paid for everything in that kitchen. The pots imported from Provence. The Sub-Zero. Even the damn lentils. There was no need to feel awkward. But she did and when she rubbed her hands on her cotton shirt, she left a mark.

Clem and I just got a whole buncha new flavors.

That's just great, Suzanne. Mix it up a little.

But it wasn't. Great. Accepting the offer, Althea hadn't given a thought to what a challenge this would be.

First off, she needed a mug. She thought Suzanne might hop up and get her one, but the girl was just sitting there, drinking tea, picking at her split ends. Althea didn't really see how, after everything Suzanne had done for her and Clem, she could pull rank and tell her to get her a mug. Both Suzanne and Clem would think she was a total princess or, worse, a bitch. The real problem wasn't that she didn't want to get her own mug. It was that she couldn't. She didn't know where the majolica ones were and was too embarrassed to ask.

She knew there was only so long she could stand there without looking like an idiot. She opened a cabinet door and didn't find them, lost her nerve, and started to go back up to her room. But she felt the sting of the Paula fiasco of the night before and was determined to follow through. So she decided on another tactic. She turned to the table where Clem and Suzanne were sitting, picked up the teapot, which, thank God, was almost empty, carried it to the sink, boiled some more water, and filled it; that seemed more industrious and competent than getting a mug. She brought the pot back to the table.

Suzanne had gotten up to change the classical station to carols, which Althea hated. The loop of self-righteous messianic songs irritated her, to say the least; sometimes she feared they would bring on an episode of the Visions. But tonight, Althea was so focused on her failure to find a mug and on being with Clem and Suzanne that she barely noticed the music; she hoped Suzanne would bring back a mug.

Suzanne returned empty-handed. Althea wondered if Suzanne was trying to humiliate her by getting her to admit she didn't know where the mugs were. And then, of course, it followed that she was totally out of touch with what went on in her household. And the people who lived in it. And that it was too late to catch up. And Oliver was going to leave her (how could he not?) and take Clem and Suzanne with him. She knew that in the case of divorce, the better parent always won, got custody of the child (and the nanny). She would get the pots from Provence to make lentils in, the Sub-Zero, the mugs (wherever they were), and herself.

She knew the Clem Experiment was already a failure. She would just tell them she had to go to the bathroom, that she would be right back, and then go up to her room and stay there. They would forget all about her and she would — give up? But somehow, she hung on just a little longer, and after Suzanne added the tea bags to the pot, Althea poured tea for Suzanne and Clem.

Lune?

Yes?

Your hands are shaking. You're going to spill the tea all over yourself.

It's fine.

Why don't you sit down. I'll get you a mug, Suzanne said. Finally, Althea thought.

I'll go, Clem said. *Is it okay if I get another kind of mug? The ones we have are sort of weird.*

That would be perfect, Clem. Althea thought about slipping in a *sweetie* after the Clem but was afraid it might sound contrived. Instead, she just sat across from Suzanne. Clem scooted out of the banquette and walked over to the cabinet by the sink, one over from where Althea had looked (she had been so close!). There were three shelves of mugs in different colors and sizes. Clem pulled over a white-painted footstool and began going through them. Althea watched as she moved them around with her delicate hands, examining the handles, turning them upside down, looking at the bottoms, bringing them up to her face and — what, smelling them?

Suzanne bumped her with her elbow, and just then, she noticed a chartreuse flyer bordered in silver glitter at the other end of the table. It was so disjointed, she knew there must have been a committee behind its production. Clem detested glitter. She said it was too messy to apply and, even worse, too *obvious*. Althea had once asked Clem what she meant by *obvious*, and Clem explained: *There's nothing going on with glitter. It's just happy! Festive! There's nothing to figure out.* Althea had wanted to say that most art by nine-year-olds was probably pretty *obvious*, but she had let it go. She reached for the flyer.

Though not yet forty, she could barely see a word without her reading glasses. She squinted and made out:

Christmas Charm, Hanukkah Cheer
Come to the Fourth-Grade Mommy/Daughter Bake Sale
December 13, 9 to 11 a.m.
No caregivers, please.

The *no caregivers* made her think of the signs outside restaurants that said *We love your pets, but unfortunately the health department doesn't.* She wondered how any contraband nannies would be handled by the smug do-it-yourself mommies. Undoubtedly some women would try to sneak them in; they were as necessary to them as iPhones.

At the bottom of the glitter paper, scrawled in silver ink:

Althea and Clementine Willow:
Treat Appétit — peppermint meringues

The peppermint meringues almost pushed her over the edge. Of course, she couldn't cook. But even if she could, why peppermint meringues? They weren't even edible as far as she was concerned; they tasted like chalk with a little bit of air mixed in. Why hadn't she and Clem gotten gingerbread men, refrigerator fudge, or plain old chocolate chip cookies? But she knew. They thought meringues were out of her league. The mommies were looking forward to watching her fall down on the job in real time.

But she wasn't going to let this happen. She would Google a recipe, one of those *Ready, Set, Gourmet!* ones. The event was three days away. Surely she could pull it off.

Althea took her time finishing her tea with Clem and Suzanne. She barely said anything, just kept looking at the chartreuse piece of paper. Somehow, Clem intuited what she was thinking.

Lune? It's okay if we just blow that off. It sounds pretty lame. Treat Appétit? What does that even mean? Really. I can just miss the first part of school that day.

She was offended by Clem's assumption that she would not show up, that the idea of Althea actually being there was ridiculous.

What are you talking about? Of course we'll go.

Really? But we have to make meringues. Did you see that? Who's going to want to buy them at the bake sale?

They have almost no calories. I'm sure there will be plenty of takers.

Oh. That's a good point. Althea had no idea if this was true, but it seemed like it could be.

But they're probably hard to make.

Don't worry, Clem. Really. I'm on it.

You know we have to make, like, thirty-six.

No problem.

Clem began to scratch her arms vigorously, which the pediatrician had told Oliver was usually a sign of anxiety.

I'll help, Suzanne said. *We'll get it done.*

Althea didn't want Suzanne's help with this project. Period. *No caregivers, please.* Althea was going to pull it off this time, finally get something right. She excused herself from dinner. Or from her tea. She actually put her mug in the dishwasher. She kissed Clem on the forehead and walked up to her office.

ALTHEA WAS GOING to Google recipes for peppermint meringues, really, she was, but she hadn't been on her computer since before the hospital (she rarely got e-mail so there was nothing to check) and she wasn't quite ready to face the complications of the meringues. So Althea Googled herself.

At first, she limited herself to opening three hits. There were probably about fifteen. Nothing new, however.

Her favorite was the academic.

"The Edible Complex: Sex, Gender, and Gastronomy in the Photographs of Althea Willow," Fiona Dunne, PhD, New York University.

It was just a title for a paper given at an MLA conference; it was smushed in with three other papers and edited down from a PhD dissertation, but it pretty much summed up Althea's whole *oeuvre* to date.

Then there was the representational.

Althea Willow, April 4–11, at Liler Gallery:

Please Do Not Eat. A woman with streaks of gray in her hair and wearing a hospital gown pokes her head into a kitchen freezer filled with eggs. There is a copy of *What to Expect When You're Expecting* tucked inside too.

Please Do Not Eat II. A bistro hamburger, bun red and soggy with blood, with a tampon string hanging out of it.

Please Do Not Eat III. Yellow Jell-O in urine-sample cups with chocolate mousse around the rims passed at a cocktail party to pretty young women, the kind Oliver *went to coffee with*. Althea actually had a few of the models eat them straight from the cups just for the effect.

Helen Heard: No Bids on Althea Willow Photograph

Guess which "progressive" SoHo institute of learning refused to accept an Althea Willow print for its annual auction. Willow, who has a seven-year-old daughter at the school, offered up her *Daddy's Girl* but the auction committee co-chairs had zero appetite for the gift. Helen heard from an auction insider that "it was just too late in the day to include it alongside the other lots. Mrs. Willow has to adhere to the same deadlines as everyone else." The photo? An Adonis wearing the barest of briefs cradling a naked girl doll and gazing at her adoringly while holding a peeled banana up to her mouth. *Aww . . . ain't that the sweetest?*

READING ABOUT HERSELF on the web made her feel grounded, like she was a real photographer, a real artist, a contributor to the Willow family. Even though she had had six shows total and had sold only fifteen prints. She never made any real money working, as Oliver constantly reminded her when she was well. She wasn't sure exactly what he meant by this — if he was saying that she just wasn't very talented or that her profession was not generally a lucrative one. But she didn't care about being at the top of her field, and she wasn't doing it for the money. No, she wanted another identity waiting for her, something to go back to when she wasn't consumed by the *illness*, wrecked by the Visions or the Tombs. Even if most people called her art shocking at best, and at worst obscene, anything was better than doing watercolors in her basement or teaching flower arranging in East Hampton like a lot of other women she knew (or knew of) who had their own money and just needed an outlet, some way to plug in and get some kind of spark, however minimal. So instead of looking at just three hits, she sat in front of her computer for the next two hours and opened every site that mentioned her or Oliver. Surprisingly, not one of them made reference to her illness. In the art world, being bipolar was probably akin to being left-handed — not that unusual. As protective as Oliver was, he had never used Spectacle's PR to do damage control on her behalf. As it turned out, the only real damage she seemed to wreak was in their household.

When she went to bed that night, she'd made no progress on the meringues, but looking at all of the articles made her feel like she had officially left the hospital and was once again among the *functionings*.

Three days later, on the morning of the MDBS (Mommy/Daughter Bake Sale or, more appropriately, More Damn Bullshit), she and Clem had actually managed to make thirty-six peppermint meringues and had individually wrapped them in green cellophane with purple bows that Clem had painstakingly tied (Clem said red would have been *obvious*). She and Clem had finished the project the night before, and without any help from Suzanne; Althea had sent Suzanne to the movies so she couldn't weaken and have the nanny do the whole thing. In the end, she thought the project had actually been sort of fun. The meringues had turned out so well she was worried that the mommies would think she'd bought them. Oh, well; it was an impossible situation.

Though the school was only six blocks away, she and Clem took a town car there, which was just not *done*, as even she knew. You were expected to walk or, if you lived too far, take the subway, a bus, or possibly a cab. A town car was just *wrong*; although you lived in the city, transportation was supposed to be as consuming as if you lived in the suburbs. She guessed it was just a mommy skill, a total time kill, another notch in their victimhood. Town cars were for dads who had jobs to go to or for the occasional expats from Dubai or Venezuela who didn't know any better but would soon learn (or would transfer to international schools).

But that day, with all their confections, were Althea and Clem really supposed to stand on the corner in front of the loft and try to hail a cab? Oliver had offered to help them do it, but she refused. She was not going to have the meringues crumble by her feet, the bags tipping over in the cab as she fumbled in her purse to find her credit card.

They arrived at the school in about five minutes, so she asked the driver to circle the block a couple of times. She was suddenly nervous. She had managed to get up early enough to shower, dust on some bronzer, and throw on a floor-length purple velvet dress with cap sleeves and a pair of tan ankle boots. Before they left, she'd put on a suede jacket; her hair was still wet, so she'd pulled it back into a messy ponytail and added her favorite floppy tan hat. She knew she would be cold on the walk home, but she could grab a cab. She hadn't had time for breakfast and had downed a Diet Coke. She was now on her second. She knew she wasn't supposed to have that much caffeine with her meds, but they would have water and food at the school. She held her hands out in the town car, and they were shaking. Worse than usual. Shit.

She had been in such a rush, she hadn't taken her meds. She had brushed her teeth, put on lipstick and bronzer, but not taken her meds. She wouldn't die; she would just feel more unstable, shaky. The smart thing to do, of course, would be to go home and take them or even ask Suzanne to bring them. But since she never put them in the weekly pill case as her doctors instructed, Suzanne would have had to bring all six of the bottles, and she would have had to go somewhere to count and sort them. She knew someone would find her; wouldn't that be exciting! It was not a dire situation. It just made her feel incompetent and worried. Not at the top of her game.

Their driver completed the second loop around the block and pulled up in front of Tides. The school had been founded fifteen years earlier, which, in the New York City private-school world, was the equivalent of about five minutes ago. And since being an established or, rather, *old school* counted for almost everything, there was no getting around the newness of the Tides School, no matter how much money you threw at it. Even though the girls wore cashmere sweaters as part of their uniforms and learned four languages (including Arabic and Mandarin) and had a lab that looked like it was straight out of MIT, other parents whose children attended places whose names did not have to be repeated twice in conversation to be recognized smiled condescendingly when they found out these girls went to Tides.

Oliver and Althea knew Clem was qualified for any of the top-tier schools. She had perfect ERBs — essentially SATs for four-year-olds — and all her preschool teachers loved her, but as soon as each ebullient director of admissions reviewed the Willows' "whole package" (as the schools called it), he or she suddenly treated Clem like she was on the spectrum or, at the very least, just a notch above special needs, and Althea and Oliver were told that Clem *would definitely be a better fit else-*

where. Of course, it was just not done to ask why Clem had been rejected. After all, it wasn't like the Willows didn't already know. It was obviously Althea's fault. All schools had to take precautions. What if she volunteered to chaperone a field trip or, God forbid, give tours? And what about safety patrol? She was unpredictable (so the schools heard) and possibly even dangerous. Really, what if she went nuts when she was wearing one of those orange vests and helping the children cross the street? Any school was right to turn their family down.

After eight rejections, the Willows were desperate. Or at least Oliver was; Althea was all for public school. But Oliver complained of their plight to anyone who would listen, and finally his squash partner, Miles, told him there was a school called Tides that had rolling admissions and wasn't too far from where they lived. He even knew a board member who might be able to help. Oliver told Althea about this at dinner, trying to seem happy, but she could tell by the way he clapped his hands and clasped them together for emphasis as he talked that his cheerfulness was bullshit. He wanted to be part of the uptown party too. He wanted the nod, the invite, the place at the table.

But when a breakfast was finally set up for them with Nick, the chairman of the finance committee of Tides, Oliver acted like Tides was what he had been looking for all along for his daughter. What else could he say? Nick had been on the board of Tides for six years and had three girls at the school. He told Oliver and Althea he could surely get Clem in — if the Willows came across as philanthropic. Giving back was what the school was all about.

Oliver said of course he would write a check. *Checks. Whatever it takes.*

But Nick said, No. *That would be buying your way in. It doesn't work like that.*

What, then? Ollie was getting impatient, Althea could tell. They needed a school for Clem. All schools needed money. What game was Nick playing?

New philanthropic venture: See It Through. Cool glasses for inner-city kids. I'll do the lenses, you do the frames.

Oliver flushed. Althea knew he was furious, that he felt like Nick had tricked him. It was going to be an almost impossible project for his small boutique company. He just didn't work on that scale. Didn't want to water down the brand. But Clem had a school.

THEY GOT OUT of the car for the MDBS. Althea had tried to get Clem to wear a green crushed-velvet dress and green velvet ballet shoes, but Clem explained she needed to wear her uniform, which Althea didn't really get. She thought the school would make an exception, but then she saw other girls going in and realized she had been wrong. She took their shopping bags from their driver and could not wish him away fast enough as the mothers stared at them.

No one else was carrying bags, just Tupperware or cardboard boxes from the dry cleaner. These had a kind of homey look, as if the moms were scrounging or ad hoc-ing it, which seemed strange because the mothers at Tides certainly had enough money to buy proper, even festive containers.

The first woman Althea encountered when she entered the

school was Yancy. Clem had already abandoned her mother to find her friends. Yancy was five three and president of the Parents' Association. She was not mean, but she had no patience for anyone who got in the way of whatever her current agenda was. She was wearing a yellow and black knit dress that made her look like she should be pollinating something. The toes of her black boots were so scuffed, she must have been in the habit of kicking walls when she was frustrated.

Althea, Yancy said without looking up from the clipboard. *Peppermint meringues.*

Right. And, Yancy, your dress. It's really unique —

But Yancy wasn't interested in Althea's opinion of her clothing. She was running an MDBS.

You and Clem should set up over there. Where's your container?

We just brought a bag. I thought we could set them directly on the table.

What? The table is hardly sanitary. It's from the art room and has glue and paint on it. We cleaned it, but still —

It shouldn't matter. The meringues are wrapped.

You wrapped them? In what?

Cellophane.

Althea. This is a green school. We don't use things we can't recycle.

Althea flushed. This part wasn't on the flyer. *Well, what do you want me to do?*

The first-graders can use the wrappers for art projects.

What about the meringues?

They can eat them for snack.

But these took forever to make. I don't think first-graders even like meringues.

The teachers can eat them, then. But that's beside the point. This morning is about school spirit. Spending time with our daughters. Not about who sells or doesn't sell what.

Of course, Althea said. Or meant to say. She felt her mouth dry up and saw Yancy's face start to get blurry. She looked down at Yancy's tiny little beat-up boots and tried to distract herself by thinking about how any normal person knew when shoes hit their expiration date. And once that happened, it just wasn't something you could let go for very long. Because no matter how attractive you were, old shoes would take you down.

But mocking Yancy failed to stop what Althea knew was coming, what was worsening by the minute. She looked up, thinking maybe she would snap out of it if she focused on Yancy's face. But it just kept getting worse. She had lost almost all the feeling in her legs and was having a hard time breathing. She felt like she was going to pass out or have a heart attack. She wanted to bite Yancy's elbow to calm herself, or ask the woman to smack her in the face.

Althea hadn't had a panic attack since her twenties, had been fine since she'd started the Klonopin all those years ago. Dr. Bair always said she was very sensitive to medication, but still . . . she'd never thought missing a single dose would cause this.

Althea searched the crowd for Clem but had no idea where she was. In the bathroom? Her classroom? Althea couldn't really see at that point anyway. Everything and everyone blurred together. She knew she had to get out of there. But how? She couldn't exactly ask one of the mommies for help. The only thing that would stop the attack was some Klonopin, and she couldn't very well panhandle for benzos at the MDBS. If the mothers had some, they weren't going to admit it. The only viable solution was to hail a cab, go home, take her meds, and, maybe, return to Tides like nothing had happened. She could make the round trip in twenty minutes at most. If asked, she could say she had been waiting for the bathroom or walking around the school.

The panic attack was subsiding a bit. Althea knew they usually lasted only about ten minutes or so. But still, they were unbearable.

Yancy? Althea was frantic. She had to give a reason for leaving. But she wasn't sure she could talk.

What now?

Althea scanned the room, and a poster caught her eye.

Nuts.

Nuts? You put nuts in the meringues? Nuts are a loaded gun. Everyone knows Tides has zero tolerance for nuts.

No. I just ate one. I don't feel well.

Was it on school property?

I guess. I found it in the bottom of my purse.

I hope you washed your hands.

Yancy, I have to go.

SHE KNEW HER body was minutes from a total shutdown. She fled the school, not even bothering to find Clem and tell her she was going. She stumbled for about a block in the snow before she found a taxi that would take her. She knew she looked like she was drunk or on drugs.

Later, under the covers of her king-size bed, still fully dressed, she wondered if it had been worth going to the MDBS at all. Although it could easily have turned out differently. If she had gotten up just half an hour earlier, followed her normal routine. But she hadn't. It was just another Althea-style fuckup. But maybe this time, there was progress. For once, she realized, she was disappointed in the outcome. And she knew Clem would be too. She hadn't even said goodbye to her. If she weren't so tired from the double dose of Klonopin she had just taken, she might have gone back to Tides, but she just couldn't. Finally, the attack subsided and she fell asleep.

Althea felt a hand rubbing the top of her head gently and assumed it was Suzanne or Clem making sure she was okay. But it quickly got more forceful, and then she heard:

Althea? Aren't you supposed to be at the bake sale with Clem?

Oliver.

I had a reaction to my meds and had to come home.

Reaction? What does that mean? Did you call Bair?

Um, no.

Why not? That's part of the deal.

It wasn't necessary. I knew what the problem was and I fixed it.

Fixed it? Who gave you the green light to alter your doses?

It wasn't that.

What was it, then?

I forgot to take my meds before we left and had a panic attack when we got there.

Jesus. What about Clem?

I left her there. Althea got out of bed and stood to face him.

What?

Well, she ran off with all her friends and I couldn't find her.

So she has no idea where you are.

Oliver, you don't understand. It was horrible. I could barely see and I thought I was going to die.

Well, did you tell someone? One of her teachers? Another mom?

No. I didn't think of it.

Of course not.

In any case, it would have embarrassed her.

Althea, how is it that every time you try to make things better, you only make them worse?

Oliver, it wasn't like it was on purpose —

I know. You forgot to take your meds . . . Or maybe you remembered. Remembered that Althea doesn't make meringues. Doesn't do bake sales. Shows up but can't follow through. That doesn't count. I'm fed up, Althea. Wake up.

I feel terrible. I really do.

Well, you better start taking some responsibility. Otherwise.

Otherwise?

Otherwise.

She was completely stunned by Ollie's *otherwise*. Of course, she had recently been terrified he was *thinking* it, but he had never, ever said it. What went unsaid left a greater margin for hope, no? But now he had put it out there.

Well, Oliver, I've had it with your sideshows. Somehow, for the first time, she summoned the courage to challenge him.

That's rich, Althea. Really rich.

IF OLLIE LEFT . . . She had never loved anyone but him, had not been without him since she had been diagnosed. Who else would want to deal with that? And even if she were well, she wasn't exactly an enticing package — she was nearing forty; was obsessive, awkward, introverted; had absolutely no idea how to flirt. She hadn't been interested in sex for years. She gave Ollie the occasional obligatory blowjob, the one stipulated in all marital contracts, but that was about it. Who would want to date that kind of woman?

And she would be saddled with that horrible moniker: *divorcée*. She did have her own money and a career, which would surely be appealing to some men, but her photographs would also probably freak some out, make them think she was a pervert. She supposed if all else failed, there were those bipolar dating websites. *Meet Compassionate Singles Who Don't Let Being Bipolar Stop Them from Finding Love.* They would joke about them in after-care.

No, she couldn't even entertain the possibility of Ollie leaving her. It was unbearable. But it hadn't come to that yet. She would get it together. Make things right with Clem. Or try her best to. She was sure Oliver would give her points for trying.

| | | | | | | |

THAT WINTER AND SPRING, she really thought she was making headway with Clem. Althea's doing school drop-off and pickup were out of the question after the MDBS, but she was there when Clem and Suzanne got home for the afternoon. Well, more accurately, she was in her office pretending to work. She would hear them come in and wait for them to have a snack, and once Clem got settled in her room to do the little homework she had, Althea would poke her head in, ask her how it was going, and leave, justifying the brief visit by telling herself she wanted to be one of those mothers who checked in but didn't *hover*. It was really just easier to catch Clem when she was engaged in other things. That way it seemed like she was bothering Clem, not the other way around.

She joined Clem and Suzanne for dinner two or three times a week. She didn't eat (it was too early; she wasn't hungry; she should really wait for Oliver to come home) but she did try to participate in their conversation and sometimes (she thought) managed to come up with interesting things to say. They even started to expect her, to set out a mug for her tea. The biggest change, though, was that Clem began to talk about Althea's work, asked her to explain her photos.

At first, Althea didn't know if she should, wasn't sure that it was appropriate. She wasn't completely out of touch with what a nine-year-old should know. Sure, some of the pictures were hanging in the loft, but Althea had the absurd idea that Clem had never noticed them. As if they were as banal as the living-room rug or dining-room sconces. But of course Clem would be curious.

Well, Clem, what do you think they are about? She deflected the question, wanting to see what Clem thought before she started explaining.

Loneliness.

Loneliness?

You always photograph people alone. Even when there is more than one in the shot, they still don't look at each other. No matter what, it's like they are always by themselves.

That's an interesting way of looking at it. Althea had never thought of it that way.

None of them are happy.

Well, you may have a point there, but in most cases in art, happy is boring. Happy doesn't sell.

Is that why you don't take pictures of me? I'm not happy all the time, you know.

Clem, I don't take pictures of you because I don't want strangers looking at you.

But don't you want to have something to remember me by when I'm older?

I already do, Clem. Your baby teeth, drawings from school, monogrammed baby pillows. This was a lie. She had thrown those things away a long time ago, telling herself it was because she hated clutter.

But still . . . Clem said.

The truth was, Althea didn't take pictures of people she knew. Familiar people took away her objectivity, broke through her boundaries, and ultimately grabbed control of the shoot, which overwhelmed her. Of course, this wasn't the case with most professionals, but it was with her. This precluded even a simple Christmas-card photo, which infuriated Ollie.

You're a photographer, for God's sake. What's the problem with taking one picture of Clem and sending it out to our friends like everyone else with a kid does? "Merry Christmas from the Willows"?

She knew she couldn't photograph Clem. But she could always promise to. After all, a promise was often just a place-holder for something that didn't work out.

Sure, Clem. Of course I can do a shoot with you.

CLEM'S BIRTHDAY WAS near the end of March. She was turning ten. Althea thought she might throw her a party (she could hire a service to help her and still get all the credit; that's what everyone else did), but Clem liked only two of the girls in her class. Althea offered to take them to a play, let them spend the night at the natural history museum, whatever, but what Clem wanted was to go out to dinner with Ollie and Althea at Sushi Yasuda, one of the most expensive sushi restaurants in New York and also one of the best.

After the three of them ordered, Clem produced a list written on onionskin paper. It consisted of three items neatly calligraphed in blue-gray ink. (She liked to ask for, rather than receive, presents on her birthday.)

Day Break Equestrian Camp
Redecorate my room in East Hampton
My own horse

Oliver, always the granter of wishes, said, *Yes to camp. Yes to a room redo. Hmm to the horse. What about the fall, when we're back from East Hampton? What will we do with it then? Not sure what NYC garages charge for horses.*

I could ride it to school, Clem said. *Lune could ride it home. Seriously, we could board it somewhere warm like Florida and I would fly down and compete.*

This just keeps getting better and better, Clem. Oliver laughed.

You always say I'm an original. This is original.

Hardly. Every little girl wants a horse.

But not every girl has a daddy cool enough to get her one.

Ha. Clever. I'll think about it. Althea? Are we on the same page?

She had been too busy considering how easy the summer would be with Clem spending the days at riding camp to listen to the rest of their conversation. She could let the summer girl handle the drop-offs and pickups and most of the weekend activities; she could join in when she felt like it and finally get back to work. She had made no headway this winter.

Sure. Of course. Clem's going to love it.

But Clem, even with the first two, pony camp and the room redo, there are going to have to be cutbacks.

She and Clem looked at Oliver incredulously. He had never been cheap. And as far as they knew, Spectacle was having a great year.

Such as? Althea said, trying to sound calm when she really wanted to scream, What the hell are you talking about? She knew something big was coming, but what?

Since Clem is going to spend all day riding, we won't need a summer girl in East Hampton this year. You can use Lola oc-

casionally if you need her, but having a live-in would just be overkill.

Lola was the daughter of their housekeeper, Coco. Sure, she was usually available, and she and Clem got along, but she was a part-time babysitter and not a nanny. Althea would have to think ahead, make arrangements if she wanted Lola to come. She would be alone with her daughter most of the time. Yes, Clem would be at camp, but they were going to East Hampton at the end of May and camp didn't start until mid-June. And Oliver came out only on the weekends. But what could she say? *That's the worst idea I ever heard? No.*

Then she remembered the decoration project. Clem wanted her room redone. Why not redecorate the whole East Hampton house? Maybe even start by sprucing up the loft in the city? That would give her and Clem something to do, something to talk about, something Ollie could be proud of. She would need help, a decorator, but she and Clem would be in charge. Of course, Althea cared nothing about fabrics and light fixtures and drawer pulls, but she knew that since she had a house on Lily Pond Lane, one of the most affluent areas in town, and a large disposable income, she was supposed to.

CLAIRE BISSOT HAD been a designer at Spectacle for about two years. She was thirty-two and French; worse, she was Parisian. That meant she was cultured and chic and, well, *you weren't.* Althea had barely told Ollie her plans for remodeling Lily Pond when he said he would *lend* her Claire, like she was some kind of company car, to manage the project.

The few times Althea had met Claire, at Spectacle Christmas parties or work dinners, she had absolutely despised her. Claire was too blunt to inspire confidences, plus she could tie an Hermès scarf and not look like a stewardess and apply liquid eyeliner. Althea didn't normally care about these things, but because Claire did them so well, all of a sudden they seemed very important. The worst thing about Claire, however, was her sense of humor. Or lack thereof. She laughed, but it was just meanness with sound. And even when it wasn't explicitly directed at her, she somehow came away from the exchange humiliated.

Claire had dark hair like Althea did, but it was inky black to her dark brown, and Claire's everyday look was a tight chignon. Althea never managed anything tight with her unruly hair; messy knots or braids were as far as she got. But Claire's hair was irrelevant compared to Claire's face. Or Claire's Face, as Althea thought of it. It deserved to be a proper noun; it was art. It was sublime, transcendent. Claire's Face infuriated her.

Claire's eyes were green, a dark green that didn't change no matter what color clothing she wore or whether she was in sunlight or shadow. Claire was obdurate; why shouldn't her eyes be too? She had a medium-size mouth, in perfect proportion to the rest of her face, and tumescent lips that looked like someone had punched her (how Althea wanted to be that person) and the swelling had never gone down. If Claire were American, one might have suspected a collagen injection, but Althea knew that the French loathed anything remotely adulterated — vanilla ice cream with chunks of cookie dough mixed in, jeans with spandex, even coffee with hazelnut creamer.

Claire was taller than she was by about two inches, five in

the stilettos she cruised around in with such agility she seemed to be barefoot. Claire's leg muscles were so developed they cut deep into the backs of her calves, which was another gross injustice since Althea was confident that Claire (again, being French) never sweated through a spinning class, pounded out those imaginary miles on a treadmill, or posed her way into yogic bliss.

She couldn't figure out if Oliver was oblivious to the fact that she detested Claire or if he realized it and didn't care. She had to know what her husband was thinking.

Oliver, I haven't seen any of Claire's work. We can't just go ahead and hire her. This was her being reasonable.

Claire's one of the best designers I have. And, seriously, Althea, you've never even read a shelter magazine. This was Oliver being condescending.

I don't need magazines for inspiration. Besides, Claire works on sunglasses. That has nothing to do with interiors. And this is my project. I should choose who I get to work with. This was her standing up for herself.

Good taste is good taste. She's got loads of it.

But this is a huge job. This is our house, Oliver. Shouldn't we at least look at a few people?

You know I go by gut. Plus we know her already, and she is going to live with us, after all.

Huh?

To oversee the project.

Somehow, this had never occurred to her. Was she an idiot? How many weeks of hell would that be? Eight? Twelve? She honestly didn't know.

I'll think about it.

There's nothing to think about. It's done. I've hired her. This was Oliver being a dick.

Oliver...

You'll see I'm right. Don't worry.

Fine. Althea knew Ollie never went back on his word. Claire it was.

SO SHE ACQUIESCED (she really had no choice, did she?) and started working with Claire on the warm-up project on the loft she had devised. After Althea had spent about three weeks with Claire sifting through paint samples and fabrics, Claire's Face actually became less of a knockout, maybe because she got used to it, or maybe because they had a shared goal, common ground. Claire didn't seem to pick on her as much; she deferred to Althea and let her make choices, maybe since she knew she was coming to East Hampton to live with them for a while. Claire even became less hard, less French, and not a few times, Althea caught her staring off into space, daydreaming and even smiling to herself. She came to see why Ollie had hired Claire and overridden her objections.

Claire did a brilliant job, totally reconfiguring the loft in a way Althea never could have imagined. In six weeks, they had the walls painted aubergine, new sofas upholstered in gray velvet, Lucite stools, and Althea's work mounted everywhere. They even hung a swing, made out of wood from Oliver's childhood tree house, in the middle of the living room. It was not sturdy enough for even Clem to sit on, but still, it gave the impression that Althea was whimsical rather than disorganized, that she was even kid-friendly.

One night Claire joined them for dinner. Afterward, while Ollie read *Catch-22* to Clem before bed, the two women sat in the living room drinking espresso and discussing Althea's photographs. Claire had changed out of her tailored navy crepe de chine suit into one of Ollie's waffle robes that Althea had dug out of a basket in the laundry room. Claire said she hated to get her clothes wrinkled after she was done working for the day, but Althea had noticed that Claire's skirt was a little tight. Finally, life was fair — even Frenchwomen bloated when they got their periods. Claire would never admit to suffering such an indignity, of course, would never ask Althea if she could borrow a Tampax.

If pressed, Claire might have blamed the skirt's snugness on the Key lime pie they had had for dessert. Not on herself for having eaten the pie, but on the pie itself, as if it had malfunctioned by making her feel full. Althea knew, however, this was not the issue; she had seen Claire eat precisely three bites, and she'd had to gag them down at that. The robe was huge on her and solved the problem, but Althea felt a bit uneasy that Claire seemed so comfortable wearing her husband's clothes.

Claire was smoking Marlboro Reds, one after the other, as if they were providing oxygen, not depriving her of it. Althea was tempted to join her, but Ollie always said it was a trashy habit and especially deplorable when mothers did it. Althea remembered being in Paris and seeing not only *mamans* pushing strollers smoking but women who must have been nine months pregnant. Althea couldn't understand how they, or even Claire (Oliver had spent five minutes finding her an ash-tray), got away with it. Between what must have been cigarettes nine and ten, after not really talking much, Claire said:

You say you take photographs, *but you really more like* make *them, no? They are very arranged. Like flowers.*

By *arranged*, did Claire mean "static"? Or did she mean "conceptual"? Despite having been in the States for over seven years, Claire still spoke in translation. But Althea didn't want to ask for a clarification in case it turned out Claire was being critical.

They were looking at her latest series, *Take This and I'll Call You in the Morning: The Dystopia of the Female (Anti-)Body*. The photos featured a big-chested girl wearing a sheer white T-shirt that said BLOW MY MIND! and plain white cotton underwear, simple and innocent, like Clem's. In the first photo, the girl was lolling on her back in a tan-carpeted hallway, sucking on a thermometer like it was an icicle. A man wearing a surgical mask, latex gloves, and green scrubs held out an enormous flesh-colored dildo and a fistful of bobby pins; he seemed to be waving the pins in the direction of her stomach, which was just inches away from a wall socket.

So now the girl had a tough decision. Should she impale herself with the rubber (what — wand? gross plastic thing?) until her eyes rolled back in her head? Or thread the small metal ribbons into the electric outlet, fry herself to flatline? (Why? Because she could? Because the sparks flying from the wall might look cool? Because extreme physical pain is the antidote to sadness, boredom, stupidity?) Maybe the girl would play with the dildo and then move on to the pins? Maybe she'd ignore both? Maybe she would chat with the man, or shove the dildo in his ass, or stab the pins in her hair, or take a nap, or have a cigarette, or all of the above. Or maybe none of the above.

But that wasn't the point. The point — the reason Althea took photographs, that she was an artist — was to show that everyone's situation, everyone's present, contained infinite options. At that very time on that very day, you could masturbate, kill yourself, play with your hair. But none of those choices got you anywhere, as in getting you from point A to point B to point C. You were always at point A. Having to choose again. And again. *It was all the same fucking day, man.* No wonder Althea got depressed.

Then Claire said:

Where are the photos you must take of Clem? She is so very beautiful, surely you do this, no?

Of course Claire wasn't accusing her of anything.

But still Althea said (like Claire's opinion counted for something):

I don't show them. They're just for our family.

It was ridiculous, really, but she wanted Claire to believe her.

THE LAST WEEKEND in May, the Willows decamped to East Hampton for the summer. The car ride was silent except for the Rachmaninoff Clem liked. As planned, there was no summer girl that year stuffed in the back with Clem, her duffle bags weighing down their knees, the trunk full; no chitchat about what out east was like, no questions about the girl's family, friends she had back home. Althea always suffered through the endless selfies the girl showed her during the drive, just to get in her good graces, make her think Althea was cool.

How could Oliver possibly have thought not having a summer girl was a good idea? They hadn't even gotten there and she felt like he had decided they would be going the whole summer without air conditioning. She wondered if maybe they could stop at the gas station in Manorville and find someone.

The Willows didn't have a guesthouse or even pool house suitable for sleeping in, so Claire would be staying with them in the main house. Althea would be confronted with Claire's Body (yes, that was a work of art too), her clothes, her books (in the original French, of course) everywhere: on the stairs, in the kitchen, in the living room, by the pool . . . She wondered what Claire slept in. She hoped the woman would bring her own damn robe.

IT WAS THE Tuesday after Memorial Day weekend. Oliver had gone back to the city to work, leaving her alone with Clem and Claire. She suddenly wondered if Claire was also there to watch her and report back to Oliver on what kind of job she was doing with Clem. But without Oliver in the house, Claire slept in, and Althea reassured herself that Claire really didn't care what she was up to. And at that moment, she was on track. She was outside by the pool waiting for Clem, who wanted to show her some of her new dives.

She was sitting on the pool's edge, legs submerged in the water to her knees. Ollie kept the pool as cool as fall rain. It was salt water, and the temperature made him feel like he was swimming in the ocean. It was such a hot day; her thighs were starting to sweat and burn. She was just about to get up and put some more sunscreen on when she was shoved in the middle of her back, just below her shoulder blades. Before she could take a breath, she was falling forward into the pool, smacking her face on the still blue surface of the water. She went under, flailing, in a total panic. Althea hated to swim. Swimming meant getting wet, a clingy suit, a towel, drying off, taking a shower, drying off again, getting dressed.

Too many steps, even when she wasn't depressed. But even worse, she wasn't sure what she was supposed to do in the pool. Laps reminded her of pacing, moving but going nowhere, and while she swam, instead of thoughts, broken pieces of feelings came up, and the whole process made her completely anxious.

And not doing laps, just being in the water, hanging out, was almost as bad. She could go in for a quick dip to cool off, sure, but anything longer than three minutes brought up existential quandaries: What was she doing there? What was the point? She could almost hear Ollie say, Because it's fun. But why was this supposed to be fun? Because it is. It's play. But she absolutely didn't know how to play. Even if she was doing something where someone kept score, she always got that existential (that word again) boredom and couldn't wait to be done. Tanning might have seemed equally pointless, but she could handle it. When she was tanning, she could sleep, read, eat, or talk to Ollie. But right now, she wasn't tanning. She was out of her element. Her comfort zone. She wasn't drowning exactly, but she was in the water.

She touched the bottom and kicked her way back up.

Fuck! she yelled as soon as she broke the surface.

Surprise! Clem was laughing like it was the biggest, best joke ever. Althea didn't want to shout at her, but she was pissed. How many times had she told her not to push her in? Ollie loved it, but Clem knew it made her hysterical. She really wished she could get in one more *Fuck!* but she knew how much Clem hated swearing, and, after all, it was over now. Althea wanted nothing more than to get out, change into a dry cover-up, sit in the hammock with some iced tea, and maybe read a good book or, God forbid, a shelter magazine.

But the whole reason she had been sitting out here waiting was to spend the morning with Clem. And she couldn't even be with her for two minutes without losing it.

Clem was standing right above her on the deck in her too-small pink-and-white-striped terry-cloth cover-up. It hit at the middle of her thighs, and the sleeves came to just above the elbow. Her body was still all bones and a tiny bit of padding, and she tripped over her coltish legs all the time. She tilted her head to the left so severely, her hair was constantly covering up her face. Clem had convinced Suzanne to chop her thick blond hair to a bob because she just wasn't a bows-and-barrettes kind of girl.

Clem! You know I hate that. And it's freezing in here.

Lune, I'm sure it's refreshing. Not meat-locker. Meat-locker. That's what Oliver always said whenever he came into their bedroom, right before he adjusted the thermostat. *Shit, Althea. Why do you have the air conditioning on meat-locker?* Because she liked it that way. She would turn it back down as soon as he left, but it still bugged her that he never even asked her permission. And now he had passed this horrible term on to Clem.

Before she could answer — *splash!* — Clem cannonballed into the ice floes that Althea swore were drifting on the surface of the pool. Clem almost landed right on her, was just inches away. It was a game Clem played with Oliver, Althea knew, a kind of aquatic chicken. They tried to see how close they could get without actually landing on each other. Clem's proximity didn't amuse her; it just pissed her off.

Jesus, Clem. You almost hit me.

But I didn't. That's the fun of it.

Clem pulled herself up on a pink plastic raft and put her arms around Althea's neck.

Well, it's a miracle you didn't. Althea was highly annoyed but tried to change her tone to playful. *I mean, like, a miracle right up there with Jesus walking on water.* She gave her best attempt at a laugh but still unhooked Clem's arms like they were a necklace that wasn't going to work with her dress.

Since when do you know anything about Jesus? I thought you were an atheist. You told the school I wasn't allowed to play Mary's donkey in the Christmas pageant, remember?

Knowing about something isn't the same as believing in it, Althea said, pushing the raft away. *For instance, I know you should say Mary rode an ass, not a donkey. It sounds more biblical. But anyway, we're not atheists. People who are just too lazy to give the matter any thought call themselves atheists. I'm an anti-foundationalist: I'm against dogma. Any ideology that tries to claim there is a fundamental set of principles, one path to follow.*

Clem paddled the raft toward her. She wondered if she should push her away again. Would that count as a game? Probably. So she pushed, with just a bit more force. Clem paddled back, using quicker strokes this time, and Althea got splashed again. But, thank God, Clem grabbed the side of the pool when she got close to her, anchoring the raft and abandoning the game. Even if she didn't want to get out of the pool, Clem still wanted to have a conversation. Althea could work with that.

I don't understand. Can you give some examples?

Fortune cookies. Hallmark cards.

Why?

Because they dictate what to do, believe, feel.

What else?

Ikea furniture. Weight Watchers. Subway announcements about sick passengers.

Why?

Dogma.

Dogma? What's dogma?

A set of rules. One way of doing things. One set of fixed principles.

What about pandas? Clem's stuffed panda was named Hapgood. Althea had bought it for Clem during one of her episodes of the Visions, along with a great many other things panda. She had been reading the Stoppard play at the time — she had been reading all of Stoppard's plays at the time, simultaneously, but only the female roles — and had become convinced that Heisenberg's uncertainty principle was just the thing she needed in order to solve the Oliver infidelity problem. Because she had so many other big ideas to get to first, she named Clem's panda Hapgood so she would remember to get back to this one. Clem was over the moon about the bear, didn't seemed to mind that it came ready-named, and slept with it every night.

But she never got back to the uncertainty principle or even back to Stoppard. By the time Hapgood the stuffed panda had been with Clem for three weeks, Althea had returned to New York–Presbyterian and was on impossibly high doses of Seroquel and Zyprexa to stop the hallucinations, so sedated that she slept for three days straight. If anyone had asked her then about Heisenberg, she might have said it was a city, a river, a beer . . . she just didn't know. Even now, years later, she hated all things Hapgood: the bear, the play, the way the name sounded when you said it. Hapgood had become a concept; it represented the cruel chimera of mania. Where did all of those gorgeous, perfect, genius thoughts go? All of the intellectual ecstasies she had experienced, which were almost better than the physical ones she'd had? She really had no idea. It was all Hapgood. But Clem still loved her panda, and even Althea knew enough not to throw him away.

Althea wasn't sure what pandas had to do with anything. But she said, *Yes to pandas, Clem. But only stuffed ones. Rob Pruitt pandas, pop-art pandas, definitely not.* Even though Pruitt would argue his were antirepresentational. She knew she was getting a bit esoteric here even for Clem, but Clem seemed to be following along. Maybe she could tell Clem to get out of the pool so they could continue the conversation in the living room, cozy in robes, after stripping off their wet things and taking hot showers at the pool house? But she believed deep down she had already lost the right to tell Clem what to do.

What about maps, directions? Clem asked in a serious voice.

Now Althea was stuck. She knew how important maps and directions were to Clem and didn't want to dismiss them as more dogma; it would upset her. But she couldn't lie just to make the world okay for Clem. Besides, wasn't Althea already used to disabusing people of what they believed? Wasn't that the whole point of her work, what she did when she wasn't sick — to shock, disturb people with new truths? To force them outside their comfort zones? And those who couldn't take it, those people who said her work was indecent and offensive — she knew they lived sad little lives; she knew they were doomed.

Still, she wasn't really an anti-foundationalist. She liked the concept of it, but it was exhausting to think about more than once or twice a year. She wasn't even sure she understood it, and she knew she was inventing a lot of it as she went along. She thought she had some good points, but most of it was probably bullshit.

Water had started to pool in the pockets of the pink raft. The sun had slipped behind a cloud, and Clem had goose bumps as pronounced as her mother's. If Althea waited long enough to answer the question, kept putting it off, maybe Clem's lips would turn blue and she would have to get out? But Clem would wait all day if she had to. So Althea cut to the chase and told her ten-year-old daughter something she might well have been making up (and what *was* anti-foundationalism, anyway? Althea had to admit she was most likely getting it all wrong).

Sorry, Clem. Maps and directions are one person or team's interpretation of the earth, park, whatever. Once a map is finished, it doesn't evolve. And there is always more than one way to go. See what I mean?

You're wrong. I still think they are fascinating. I don't care what you say.

Clem sat up, pulled herself to the side of the pool, sat on the ledge, and kicked water in her mother's face.

You might think you're some big intellectual, but I think you're just full of yourself. And mean.

Althea swam over to the ladder, got out of the pool, and decided to give Clem the win. She was actually proud of her. She put her hands on Clem's shoulders and said:

Bravo, Clem. You got it. In the end, what other people think of your opinions doesn't matter.

Clem shrugged her off and tried to push her hands off her shoulders and stand up. But Althea wouldn't let go. Somehow, she believed that if she kept her sitting there, they could work it out.

Clem pushed just hard enough against her grip to stand up, but then she lost her balance and tripped on the blue slate. She broke her fall with her hands but scraped her knees and screamed, *Cantaloupe*, the fruit she hated most and hence her worst invective.

While Althea was relieved that Clem's new unhappiness had nothing to do with her (well, not really), she still felt bad. Being wet was worse than almost anything, much less being wet with scraped knees. Althea ran to get the pomegranate-colored towel from where it lay folded on one of the chaise longues and returned to Clem, who flinched as she draped the towel around her. Just as she was trying to figure out an approach that would mollify Clem or, better yet, make her forget the whole incident, Althea heard the screen door to the house slam.

Salut! Claire said, waving furiously, like she had just spotted them in a crowd. She was wearing an enormous black straw hat that cast shadows over her body and obscured her face, but not enough so that Althea couldn't make out the lime-green Spectacle sunglasses she had on, which belonged to Althea. The glasses lived on the front-hall table with the car keys, the stack of mail that hovered between junk and personal they never got around to opening, and the random objects that were just this side of useless but never got thrown away: used golf pencils, a paperweight in the shape of a daisy Althea's bank had sent for Mother's Day, one riding glove of Clem's.

Even though Althea never wore those glasses (she preferred the six-dollar purple ones she'd gotten from a street vendor in the city), Claire's helping herself to them completely pissed her off. Althea wanted to say something about it, or maybe remind her that this wasn't the South of France and it was okay to speak English.

She left Clem and approached Claire. *Sorry*, Althea said. *We were just getting out.* She tried to sound as ebullient as possible, as if she and Clem had been having the very best time in the pool.

I try to avoid chlorine. Bad for the skin.

She wouldn't tell her it was a saltwater pool. She didn't need to see her lower herself gracefully into it, her boobs bobbing about. Then she wondered if Claire was making some kind of comment about her own skin. She let it go.

So we should start thinking about the house, no? Althea asked. *We've done nothing.* Althea wanted to remind her that for all her pool chic, Claire was there to work.

Oh, I have. I've come up with a color scheme for the master bedroom and have ordered some fabric samples. I have a meeting with an antiques dealer next week just to see inventory.

Wait. We're supposed to work on this together. Like we did on the loft.

It's just that this is a bigger project.

Still. You can't just go ahead —

Oliver said — well, maybe this isn't for me to say, but he told me that you . . . comment on dit . . . you lose focus and I should just let you come in and out as you want.

But you didn't even tell me you were starting.

I thought I would let you get settled in.

That's for me to decide.

Fine.

And, Claire?

Yes?

This is my deal, not Oliver's. Okay? You report to me.

I think you have the wrong word.

Well, maybe. But you know what I mean.

Claire didn't answer. Instead, she sat down in a chaise longue and changed the subject.

Althea, why is the petite *just sitting by herself over there? Does she want to join us?*

She is a big thinker. Loves to be alone. Worries me sometimes. But I'll get her. She walked to the side of the pool where Clem still sat in the position she had left her.

Clemmie, she said gently as she approached. She had never called her this and immediately regretted it. You have to earn the right to call someone by a nickname, otherwise you sound ridiculous.

Let's get you dried off and go to BookHampton. Clem loved

to read, of course, and they certainly weren't going to hang around with Claire and her *Breakfast at Tiffany's* hat, but she wasn't sure Clem was going to let her off the hook that easily. She wrapped the towel tighter around Clem's shoulders, began to rub her back and arms, but before she could get any further, Clem said:

Could you please just stop touching me? She yanked herself away from Althea's hands so fast that Althea smacked herself in the chest. Claire was sitting right there and would probably tell Ollie about the whole thing. *Or else. Or else.* Althea looked and saw Claire was drinking Althea's iced tea while wearing Althea's shades, head tilted back under that tentlike hat, probably thinking her spiteful French thoughts: She says *I* should report to *her.* The woman can't even manage her own child.

She stepped back from Clem, let the towel fall around her. Maybe it wasn't the worst thing to let her stay by the pool a little while and calm down. Althea could go inside the house until Clem came to find her and admitted she really wanted to go to BookHampton after all.

Fine, Clem. You win, she said tersely and walked toward the door. Clem said nothing, but when Althea passed Claire, she sat up, grabbed her by the shoulder, and whispered in her ear, *You're going to leave her there, really? She must be cold.* Althea was sure she was thinking, See why I need to order the doorknobs by myself?

She's ten, that's all. You wouldn't believe her moods. Sometimes it's best just to let them have some space.

Claire raised an eyebrow. *I think I am good at children. Let me see if I can make her feel better.*

Claire walked right over to Clem, knelt down beside her,

and spoke quietly in her ear. Clem rolled her eyes at first but then began nodding almost enthusiastically. This surprised Althea because Clem wasn't one to give in easily. Claire carefully took the edges of the towel and bundled Clem up in it like she was six.

How did she know how to do this? Claire, with her high heels, tight skirts, and chignons? Did every woman but her have some kind of *touch* with children? Claire dried Clem off, and now they were holding hands as they walked — no, more like skipped (*nauseating* was the only word for it) — toward her.

The only thing that kept Althea from feeling like the most inadequate mother — actually, the most inadequate *woman* — in the world was that she'd just noticed (and she was positive she wasn't making this up out of spite) a small roll of fat on Claire's stomach, a paunch she hadn't seen beneath the robe that night in the loft. A paunch meant Claire would have to adjust her personality a bit, be nicer to people, make an effort. She might want to consider getting some female friends, who, unlike men, wouldn't care how her body looked. If she got a husband, it would obviously be a man on round two, but a long-divorced one; she would not be the woman he left his wife for. Someone might fall in love with her, but it would not be the passionate kind of love. All because of the foreboding paunch.

Clem let go of Claire's hand and sat down on Althea's chaise longue. She picked up a brush from the pool table and began brushing her hair. It was so short, she kept hitting her cheek, leaving a mark.

I'm feeling like I need some sun cream.

Althea hadn't even sat down. She wasn't expecting Claire to hand off Clem so quickly.

It's in the wicker basket in the living room.

Superbe. Claire went into the house.

Clem? I'm sorry. Really. Althea realized she would have hated herself too if she had been the one subjected to a random anti-foundationalist tirade, most of which was built on shaky reasoning at best.

I know, Lune. One of her bathing-suit straps was crooked and Althea tentatively reached over and fixed it. Clem let her.

Want to get cleaned up and go into town?

There's a new map book, To the Ends of the Earth, *that I want. Can we see if they have it?*

Sure, Clem. Yes to maps. We can check. If it's not there, I'm sure they can order it.

Thank you, Lune.

So, let's get changed.

Okay.

And Coco has a list of things she wants us to get from Round Swamp, Althea said. *We have to pick up a pie, some guacamole, and some other stuff I can't remember. You go get the list while I dry my hair. It won't take long, I promise. And if you're ready before I am, you can get a snack from Coco.*

Clem loved Coco. She had been with them since Clem was three. Althea knew time in the kitchen with Coco would make Clem wait just a little longer. Just then Claire slammed back out onto the patio, clearly having listened to their conversation, since she said, *Clem, after you visit the kitchen, come to my room. I have a little gift for you.*

Althea didn't worry about the gift; the French usually had good taste, but it was pretty traditional. She was sure Clem would be polite but then forget about whatever it was soon as Claire left.

Very thoughtful of you, Claire.

Ten minutes later, she was sitting in the Range Rover waiting for Clem. Where was she? And what was Claire's gift? Suddenly, she was dying to see it.

After another five minutes, Clem finally ran down the front stairs. She was wearing a white sundress and silver Jack Rogers sandals (the gift, Althea surmised). Chic, but ubiquitous. Althea didn't have a problem with the shoes, per se, but she had tried to buy a pair for Clem once, and Clem had adamantly refused, saying, once again, they were *obvious*. But as soon as Clem got in the car, Althea saw that the shoes were only part of the gift.

The real present was around Clem's neck: a glass pendant circled with black diamonds and filled with sand. Althea was outraged. First of all, she thought it was the coolest necklace she had ever seen. Second, she knew Clem thought it was the coolest necklace she had ever seen too. Third, she had never gotten Clem anything this amazing in her whole life. Ollie always bought the gifts.

Clem was beaming and touching it, shaking it in her hand.

Look what I got, Lune! Look!

I thought you hated jewelry.

This is different.

How?

It has meaning.

And what is that, exactly?

The sand is from Atlantic Beach. Atlantic was Clem's favorite beach in Amagansett, the next town over from East Hampton. She went there often with Ollie to collect sea glass.

It's beautiful. But you can't keep it.

Why not? Why not, Lune?

Because I can't look at it every day and think about how Claire knows what you like and I don't.

It's too expensive.

She said it was custom-made. It's not like she can take it back.

Well, I hope you said thank you.

Of course.

She knew Clem would wear the thing every day and she would have to pretend it didn't matter, and it would be one more item in her radical-acceptance column. Then there was the fact that the bitch hadn't gotten her anything to thank her for the extended stay.

Clem settled herself in the passenger seat and they pulled out onto Lily Pond Lane and headed to town. The town itself was composed of two streets, Newtown and Main, but you could easily spend twenty thousand dollars in an afternoon if you wanted to. Althea pulled into the municipal parking lot, which permitted a stingy two hours of free parking, and they hit Starbucks for Frappuccinos and pound cake before ambling next door to BookHampton. Almost everyone did this, which was a terrible strategy, since the store made you leave your drinks on a stool so crowded with plastic cups, they all threatened to fall.

As they walked over to check out the new fiction, Althea took Clem's hand. She felt a little awkward doing this; how long was she supposed to hold it? Was she supposed to squeeze it or just let the fingers sit loose in hers? When a gray-haired woman in a Lilly Pulitzer shift and a headband standing next to them by the books asked Althea to recommend a juicy beach read, she dropped Clem's hand and invented a title, just because she felt like it.

Althea walked to the counter to ask about the map book. She told the boy working there the name of it as best she could remember and then turned to ask Clem if that was right, but she was not behind her. Althea scanned the store and didn't see her. BookHampton was as small as a local bar; it had hardwood floors, books, booksellers, and customers, and that was it — there was no clutter, no gilded notebooks to inspire would-be writers, no random stuffed animals, postcards, poetry magnets. She had the sinking feeling that Clem had simply left.

But then she saw her. Clem came down from where they kept the classics, on the second floor. Well, it wasn't really a second floor; more of a loft with a walkway and a ceiling so low that you sometimes had to kneel to reach things. She was so relieved she almost clutched her chest. She had imagined Ollie calling that night:

Can I talk to Clem?

Um, she's busy.

Doing what?

She didn't say.

Well, interrupt her. It can't be that important. I want to talk to her.

Well, it's Claire. She's with Claire. I think they're working on her room.

That's good. But still.

You know, Claire's great. I'm really happy with her.

Althea, what the fuck is going on? I want to talk to Clem.

She's not here. I told you.

No, you didn't. You said she was with Claire.

She is. They just went out on an errand.

I'll call Claire on her cell, then.

Seriously, Ollie, they're working.

Seriously . . . I'm calling —

Actually, she's not with Claire. She's at the movies.

And on and on it would go. Until he got it out of her. You get only so many lies before you dig yourself right into the truth. But there Clem was, safe in BookHampton, carrying two fat tomes. *Clarissa? Middlemarch?* Althea considered people who lugged books of that size around pretentious, knowing they never actually read the books, just wanted everyone to think they did and be impressed by how intellectual they were. But she knew Clem — whatever it was she picked, she would see it through.

Whatcha got, Clem?

Moby-Dick.

Two copies? Althea thought maybe Clem had come up with an activity for both of them. She had never gotten through it in college, but she would certainly try this time. How hard could it be?

I thought Daddy and I could read it this summer. When we finish, we could sail from Sag Harbor to Block Island. Of course — Oliver loved to sail. She tried not to look disappointed.

That's quite the challenge. Are you allowed to skip chapters?

Of course not, Lune. That misses the whole point.

Can I come along on the trip anyway?

Sorry. No offense.

None taken. Of course there was. But she had turned down most of Oliver's offers to sail. He expected her to actually help crew, and she couldn't keep all the jibs and jibes straight. She just wanted to hang out and enjoy the view.

The boy behind the counter was getting impatient. There was a line. Lilly Pulitzer Shift touched Althea on the elbow and whispered she couldn't find her book rec in the store but she would definitely get it on Amazon. A woman in pristine tennis whites had eight copies of a roman à clef on the East Hampton social scene pressed against her chest. Althea guessed the woman must be the author. The man behind her ardently flipped through *Happiness Is a Chemical in the Brain.* She wanted to tell him, No, happiness is a fistful of pills. She turned back to the checkout guy and started to ask about the map book again when Clem handed her the *Moby-Dick*s and said:

It's fine, Lune. I really only want these.

But it's not a problem. You can have all of them.

But I really don't want it. Thanks, though.

And Althea heard: No, thanks, Lune. I'd rather do something with Daddy.

THE NEXT DAY, knowing Clem would be up at seven as usual, Althea set her alarm in order to join her. She took the blueberries and strawberries Coco had washed and cut from the fridge and made a fruit smoothie for Clem, pretty much the apex of her culinary skills. (Ollie had once complimented her

ordering skills.) She ate half an almond croissant from Mary's
Marvelous and drank black coffee. They sat at the breakfast
table on the porch, although Althea usually ate standing up at
the island. She was going to spend the whole day with Clem.
She had even put together an itinerary.

That day was even hotter than the previous one. Althea
wore a sleeveless purple-and-green Calypso shift, and her arms
looked almost toned. Clem was wearing navy-and-scuffed-
white Superga sneakers. Althea had the same pair and was
tempted to put them on but then thought that trying to match
Clem might make her look ridiculous. It didn't occur to her
that this gesture might make Clem happy.

Of course she was not going to attempt to swim with Clem
again — even with her new resolve, she knew she could not
pull it off — but she was going to take Clem shopping. They
could do something together at the house afterward: read, or-
ganize Clem's room, talk about what renovations they wanted
to make. The next day, they were going to sit down with Claire,
map out a timeline for work on the house, and review what she
had done already.

They went into town, to Steph's (Don't Touch My) Stuff for
puzzles and back to BookHampton for movies (even though
they had Netflix): *To Rome with Love, Supersize Me, Incep-
tion, This Is Not a Film.* Clem loved Woody Allen, hated fast
food, and liked Leo DiCaprio, and the fourth movie had been
directed by a friend of Althea's from NYU. Althea was grateful Clem didn't like American Girl movies, *Gossip Girl,* or
Pretty Little Liars. Or at least, Clem had never seen them, so
she didn't know to ask. Then they went to Bonne Nuit. She
picked out a beige cashmere wrap for evening walks on the

beach for herself and got a navy-blue one for Clem — what was better than cashmere? As she went toward the counter to pay, something caught her eye. It had been at least fifteen years, but once again, she could confidently take it off the rack and ask to try it on. Her T-shirts were baggy over her stomach. There was space between her thighs when she put her feet together. Her breasts, though on the small side, didn't sag, since she had never nursed. She was allowed. She sent Clem upstairs to try on bathing suits.

She pulled out a black teddy with garters and sheer black stockings. A blue silk baby-doll nightgown that hit at her upper thigh. A red thong with bows in the back and a matching pushup. At first, she just wanted to see what she would look like wearing them. She started out standing, turning around, then she bent over, grabbed her ankles, checked out her ass in the air. She sent Clem across the street to Dylan's Candy Bar, and after fifteen minutes of trying things on, she knew she had to buy it all. For Oliver or for herself, she wasn't quite sure.

AFTER BONNE NUIT, she took Clem to Day Spa. She hadn't had a bikini wax in about two months. It was one of those things she knew should be on her mandatory to-do list, but she never quite got to it. Wearing the lingerie with her pubes hanging out would be like wearing a couture dress with dirt under her fingernails. Even though Ollie wouldn't be back at Lily Pond until the weekend, she didn't even want to put on her bathing suit in that condition. No wonder Claire thought she was incapable of managing the house project.

Unfortunately, Clem didn't want a mani, a pedi, or any of the other spa services, so while Althea was getting the problem taken care of, Clem sat in the waiting room, bored and pouting, reading *Moby-Dick*. When Althea came to get her an hour later, Clem was on page 23.

Back at the house, they found Claire sitting on the couch, needlepointing a belt with flags on it. Althea would never have guessed Claire had a nautical side. She didn't know the flag language but hated to admit it since Oliver was obsessed with sailing, so she didn't ask what it said.

Salut! Any treasures? Claire said.

Yes! Movies, puzzles, books . . . Clem walked over to Claire and started emptying the bags. *What are you making?*

A belt for your papa. Each flag is a letter. Althea didn't like how intimate *papa* sounded.

What does it spell?

Crépuscule. *His first sailboat.*

How come Althea did not know this? And, worse, how come Claire did? Did he keep a picture of it at the office? No; she would have seen it. She couldn't imagine it coming up in conversation. Was Claire testing her? Doubtful. She would just have to fake it.

He did love that boat, Claire. I knit him some potholders with Cs on them once. As soon as she said it, Althea realized you didn't knit potholders. She wondered if she could destroy the belt or throw it away before Claire gave it to him.

We don't really knit in France.

Thank God. *What if it doesn't fit? That would be such a shame. But I should tell you, he hates surprises.*

He told me his waist size and we even went and picked out the thread together.

She was speechless. Ollie was picking out thread? With Claire? She was grateful Clem interrupted.

Did you get a gift for Lune? She loved how children were not yet embarrassed by this straightforward form of asking.

Mais oui. I left it in the car. Althea, do you want to go get it? It's a little heavy for Clem.

That was totally unnecessary, Claire.

It's just a little something. Althea was sure it was less than that.

She walked out to Claire's Mini, parked next to Oliver's Porsche. Oliver was maniacal about his car. He wouldn't even let her drive it, which completely pissed her off. She opened the back door of the Mini and saw a big cardboard box, unencumbered by wrapping paper, sloppily taped shut on the top.

She lifted it out of the car, saw the pictures on the side. It was an ice cream maker. An ice cream maker, a re-gifted one at that. She had always hated machines like this, the kind that made easy things labor-intensive. She had half a mind to leave the box in the car or take it to the garage and stick it in the trash, but she carried it into the house and put it away in the pantry. Maybe she would ask Claire to make some fucking ice cream herself.

An hour later, she and Clem were sitting on the sunporch, settled into a puzzle of the Los Angeles Freeway. Clem was locking together all of the pieces; Althea had gotten only about two. She was mostly watching, relieved she had found a project they could comfortably do together. She had even made them limeade with frozen blackberries floating in it, one of Clem's favorite drinks.

Claire had not moved from the couch; she had dozed off for about a half an hour, then resumed needlepointing. The woman couldn't talk and sew at the same time. Then Claire's iPhone beeped and she jumped up from the couch with such a burst of energy Althea hoped she was going to trip over the coffee table and hurt herself. Instead, Claire said, *I have to go to town to get something.*

She slid her feet into black silk ballet flats (no flip-flops for her) and grabbed her straw purse and a copy of *Elle Decor* from the coffee table.

Althea heard her steps on the driveway, the slam of the car door. But as Claire pulled out, Althea realized by the sound of the gravel's crunch that the car had more weight than a Mini. Claire had taken Ollie's Porsche. Oliver might not get the subtext of the used ice cream maker when Althea tried to explain it to him, but he would totally get Claire using the Porsche. When he found out what Claire had done, he would be furious. Maybe enough to fire her.

Forty minutes later, she heard the car return, a smooth glide and then a tiny splash of pebbles, like an expert skier finishing a run. She was very sensitive to sound even when she was not sick. She could tell instantly that the driver was Oliver, not Claire. She stood up expectantly.

What is it, Lune? Clem said.

Daddy's home.

Really? Clem jumped up, grabbed *Moby*, which had not left her side since they bought it, and ran to the door. Althea followed. She smoothed down her dress where it was rumpled and sweaty. She wished she had known Ollie was coming so she could have changed. Clem didn't look fresh either; her hair could have stood a brushing, she had blackberry stains on her fingers, and her toenails were dirty (when was the last time she had had a shower?), but at ten, Clem could still pull it off.

The door was shut against the A/C and it always took three good pushes to get it open. Clem was about to grab the handle to help it along, but before she could there was pushing at the door — one, two, three — and then there was Oliver, standing in front of them with two bags of groceries. His leather duffle bag was at his feet; he wore navy Vans and khaki cargo shorts. A white polo. Yellow sunglasses.

Surprise! he said.

Daddy! I missed you.

Me too. Why do you think I came back so early? He bent in to hug Clem and kissed Althea on the head as deftly as possible for someone loaded down with groceries.

She waited. She wasn't ready to say anything. She saw Claire standing right behind him, smiling shyly but proudly, like she had somehow been the one to lure him away from the office. And then she had not only nailed the timing involved in picking him up from the train but also managed the groceries. But wasn't that what *wives* were supposed to do? Althea thought. Wasn't that what *she* was supposed to do?

Claire took the bags and slid by the three of them into the kitchen. Clem followed her.

Althea was about to tell Oliver that it had been a waste to buy groceries because it was Coco's night off and she had already placed an order at Nick and Toni's when Oliver announced:

Claire's going to make dinner tonight. I told her something simple would be best. She's going to make us gazpacho, filet mignon, fresh green beans, and roasted potatoes. Althea, you can be in charge of dessert and use the ice cream maker Claire gave you.

How did you know about the ice cream maker, Ollie? she said in the most casual voice she could muster.

Claire asked me what you might like and after she insisted that, yes, she was bringing something, I said — oh, I don't remember, something about how you liked artisanal things. Tag-sale finds, for example, not scented candles or coffee-table books.

She liked *vintage*; tag sales were just other people's garbage as far as she was concerned. So Claire had possibly given her a stranger's old ice cream maker that she had rescued from his lawn for no more than ten dollars, ten whole dollars, thinking that Althea's idea of *artisanal* was throwing some mix into a machine. It just got better and better.

Yes, but how did you know? She gave it to me after you left.

When she called me and asked if I would come out.

She called you? When?

This afternoon. She said you seemed a little unfocused about the project and maybe I could help you get started.

Unfocused?

Yes. You were shopping. Tanning by the pool. Making elaborate fruit drinks.

Claire and I agreed we were going to start tomorrow morning. She was out by the pool too.

Well, did you at least get Clem what she needs for riding camp?

Not yet.

Fill out the forms?

Not yet.

Take her to the beach?

Not yet.

Jesus. Have you done one thing she likes?

We were working on a puzzle. We went swimming. And to BookHampton.

Bravo. That's about three hours of fun. I thought Claire might have been exaggerating. She always says I work too hard and I thought she just wanted me out of the office, but she was right. Your program's been a disaster. Why not send her to a riding camp that has no horses? She might have more fun.

Ollie, give me a chance.

You don't seem to understand that being a parent's about being a grownup, Althea. Doing the boring things. And it looks like the person doing those things has to be me, as usual. Just go ahead and make some ice cream with her.

SHE GAVE HERSELF ten minutes out by the pool to fume about how unfair Ollie's rant was and about Claire's gall in going behind her back. What did Claire know about being a mother anyway?

She was sure Claire's *simple* dinner (made in Althea's kitchen) would go like this: Claire would make all the sauces from scratch, pick fresh herbs and berries from the garden, and at dinnertime descend from her room perfectly dressed, while Althea would be relegated to setting the table, washing the dirt off the leaves for the salad, and pouring drinks.

Which was pretty much what happened. She wanted to pout through the whole dinner but she knew Ollie would simply ignore her if she did and pay attention to Claire and Clem, so she forced herself to join in. *Being a parent's about being a grownup, Althea.*

Claire, this is just delicious. Do you cook when it's only you? I mean, I imagine that must be kind of a big hassle, Althea said. Claire didn't take the bait.

Pas du tout. Americans are so lazy with their takeout. It's not only bad quality; it makes them fat. Clem was hanging on her every word. Althea suddenly became concerned about how Clem might take this statement.

Well, Claire, we have a saying in our family: Other people's bodies are none of our business.

I don't understand.

We don't judge what people look like. Weight is a private matter. Except Claire's paunch, of course.

No, it's not. Fat is fat. You tell people when they've crossed the line.

Don't you think fat people already know they're fat? It's not really going to be a shocker if you say something —

This is getting tedious . . . but Althea, you have lost a lot of weight, no? I remember you at the office party a few years ago. You're still not thin, but bravo. What the hell was she supposed to say to that? She didn't know, and no one else knew either, so they all just kept eating.

Then she remembered the lingerie she'd bought that day. Claire could cook all the fucking steak she wanted and make comments about her weight, but she didn't have the lingerie.

Once they were all done eating, she and Oliver cleared the table. He told Claire he would handle cleanup and she was free to go upstairs and read since it was only nine o'clock, but Claire insisted that a real cook never left the kitchen until the last spoon was dried and put away. They had taken out the wedding china and the silver, which needed to be washed by hand. Claire was horrified when Althea suggested they just rinse it and leave the rest for Coco to do in the morning. Oliver told Althea to take Clem up to bed, which he usually handled.

She hadn't put Clem to bed for ages. Or, rather, not properly. If Oliver was out and the nanny had the evening off, she would just walk Clem to her bed, turn out the light, and say good night. But she knew from hearing her with Oliver that Clem liked to chat. They walked upstairs together, side by side.

She looked down and saw that Clem's feet were literally caked with dirt.

Clem, when's the last time you had a shower?

Friday morning.

Before we left the city?

Yes. But I went swimming. Althea wasn't going to touch that one.

Don't you think it's time?

If you say so. Can I take one with you?

Althea thought standing naked in front of Clem seemed inappropriate. But she didn't want to reject her outright either.

Maybe they could take a bath together; maybe baths could be their version of reading *Moby-Dick*. A summer activity, a summer togetherness, that didn't include Claire. She could scoop the foam from the bubbles over their bodies and still remain decent. Unlike the pool, the water would be hot.

How about a bath, Clem? Would that work? Seems more relaxing than a shower.

Sure.

Sounds like a plan. Go get a nightgown. Meet you in my bathroom in five minutes.

ALTHEA STARTED THE BATH, the tub large enough for at least three, and went into her walk-in. She took off her dirty clothes, tossed them in the hamper. She went into the cabinet to get some towels. There weren't any. She looked on the back of the door for her robe, then Ollie's, but they were gone. The maid had come that day and the towels and robes must still be in the laundry room. She was about go back to her closet and grab a nightgown when Clem walked in.

Lune! What happened to you? I mean, there's nothing . . . Shit. The waxing. So much for decency. She bent over and tried to cover herself up. That didn't work so she sat on the floor and held her knees to her chest.

Clem's face was so earnest, Althea thought of saying: A small woman from Ecuador ripped off all the hair, along with a couple layers of skin, using hot green wax spread on what looked like Popsicle sticks. Yes, it was intentional. No, I wouldn't recommend it.

But Clem was only ten. So she went generic.

It's called waxing. When women get older, they generally do it.

But why? What for?

Because it gives men a more pleasant experience when they go down on you? Because they don't want to bushwhack to your clitoris? *It's just a thing in our culture. It makes you feel clean.*

What about Daddy? What will he think?

I didn't do it for Daddy. I did it for me.

I mean, no offense, but you look weird. You look like me.

All waxing isn't like this. Usually they leave some hair. A landing strip. But in a Brazilian, they go all-out. I've never had one before. I just wanted to try it. One of my friends recommended it.

Which friend? Last I checked, you didn't really have any.

Okay. That's fair. I read about it on the Internet.

Are you trying to look younger?

Why would I do that?

Well, Claire is . . .

Althea stared at her. Of all the things that made Claire so threatening, she had never factored in Claire's age. She rubbed her neck, exasperated.

First of all, if I wanted to look younger, I would get Botox or haul myself to the gym. Second of all, I don't know or care how old Claire is. She could be twenty-one or eighty. It's not an issue for me. Third, the only people who are going to see the waxing are Daddy and you.

So why?

Althea didn't say anything. The cherry bubbles in the tub smelled delicious.

Why? There must be a reason.

It's complicated.

Tell me. Tell me or I'm going to keep asking.

Supposedly the friction makes you come faster.

Lune, gross. Did I really need to know that?

Seems you did.

Okay, honestly, I thought you were going to say you were planning to photograph yourself or something.

Really. That's what you think my work consists of? Photographing my vagina?

Something like that . . .

And talking about orgasms is worse?

Kinda, yeah.

Okay. I had no idea. The bath is almost ready. Althea stood up to check the temperature, not bothering to hide her body. Clem had already seen her. There was no need to cover herself, was there?

Lune . . .

Yes? She didn't turn around, was turning the water off.

Do you mind if I take a shower in my room instead?

So she had messed up again. Honestly, she knew that you weren't supposed to say to your ten-year-old, *The friction makes you come faster.* Still, she was tired of apologizing, so she just kept fiddling with the water. She felt relieved, not defeated.

Of course I wouldn't mind.

See you in the morning, Lune.

Sure, Clem. And she got into the bath.

It was perfect. She scrubbed herself with a loofah and washed her hair with her favorite shampoo. When she got out, her skin was red from the temperature, like she had a sunburn. She started to reach for a towel and remembered that they were downstairs. She went into the walk-in and used one of Oliver's T-shirts to dry herself off. Then she saw the Bonne Nuit bag. Why not salvage the evening?

The three ensembles had cost her two thousand dollars. She decided the one Ollie would probably like the best was a sheer black pushup teddy with black garters and a black lace thong. She wasn't really sure why men liked thongs; they left marks on her hipbones and her ass hanging out, but she guessed that was the point. She attached stockings to the garters but punched a hole in one of them as she was pulling it on, so she tossed them both, leaving the garters hanging down against her pale skin like she hadn't known what she was supposed to do with them.

She wasn't sure about presentation. Should she be waiting for Oliver in bed dressed like this? Or should there be some kind of reveal, like coming out of her walk-in, letting her robe fall to the floor? She decided some buildup would be best. She would pretend to be tired when he came up, push him away, then come at him full force. Then she remembered their robes were downstairs in the laundry room. Fine; she'd sneak down the back stairs and grab them. She would put hers on right away and hang Ollie's behind the bathroom door so he could wear it after he took his postsex shower.

The laundry room was two flights down and not so much a room as a corner of the basement. It wasn't unusual for Lydia, the maid, to leave before everything was done; she came for five hours three days a week, and when her five hours were done, so was she. She had told Lydia she would pay her for the extra hours it would take her to finish, but Lydia said she had to get home to her children, so here Althea was, creeping about her own house in tarty lingerie on a hunt for robes. She opened the door to the basement, flipped on the light, went down the creaky stairs, and walked barefoot across the cold concrete toward the washing machine.

Shit, Althea thought. Lydia must have been in a real hurry because all of the clean towels and linens had been dumped in baskets, unfolded and unsorted. Althea's only option was to squat and start rummaging through the piles for the robes, which she did, wearing a black teddy and matching garters, butt cheeks exposed in a thong.

Just then she heard someone coming down the stairs. Althea grabbed a towel to shield herself and jumped up. Claire? Would that woman ever leave her alone? She forced herself to turn around. Thank God. It was Ollie.

Jesus. Oliver. You scared me. At least he was alone.

Althea? What are you doing? And what on earth are you wearing?

Something to keep you up at night. So maybe she would start early — she was sure this would grab Oliver's attention, that he would come down to get a better look, but he only stood there. Althea wondered if he just needed to see her up close, so she walked over to him. But he didn't react. It was like she had done something barely noticeable — had her hair cut two inches shorter, maybe.

And I just can't figure out how to get this thing off. Maybe you could help?

Althea reached for his collar and bent in to kiss his neck. He flinched. She was close to naked, trying to kiss her husband, and the bastard flinched.

What the hell, Ollie?

I'm sorry, Althea, but I have to ask: Are you all right?

What's that supposed to mean?

I find you digging through the laundry half naked, dressed like, well, a hooker.

I was looking for robes. I bought this stupid outfit for you. Really.

Really.

Well, your timing is impeccable, as usual. We have a house-guest. What if Claire walked in?

Why would she walk into the basement? she asked, even though five minutes earlier she had been afraid of the very same thing. *What are you doing here anyway?*

I was looking for more dishtowels. We were making do with two and it occurred to me that the rest might be down here.

Oh. Well, I guess I'll be on my way, then. Althea turned around, found her robe, and ignored Ollie as she went up to her room. She was planning to cut the lingerie into tiny pieces, but when she got upstairs she didn't have the energy, so she just threw it back in the bag. Maybe the old adage was right: you buy lingerie only at the beginning or the end of a relationship.

THE NEXT DAY was cloudy but still warm. They were supposed to work on the house, but Oliver wanted to go to the beach. She hated family trips to the beach, but she couldn't afford not to go that day. She didn't want to let Oliver know how humiliated she felt the night before. But she shuddered thinking about the packing of towels, sunscreen, snacks; the setting up of umbrellas and shovels and buckets for Clem. She had never actually done this, had only watched the summer girl and Oliver at work, and the whole thing exhausted her. When it came time to leave, Clem was upstairs looking for her flip-flops, Ollie for his Seiko Astron watch, and Claire was in the kitchen filling a ziplock bag with handfuls of cherries. Althea realized she couldn't very well just stand there, so she started packing the car alone.

They were taking the Range Rover; the Porsche and the Mini were too small. Clem came out, and several minutes later, Claire finally emerged and strode directly to the passenger side of the car, not asking if Althea needed help packing the trunk. Althea didn't really want Claire seeing her sweat-stained cover-up as she tried to jam in the last beach umbrella without impaling Clem, who was now reading patiently in the back seat, but she certainly couldn't let her ride next to Ollie. She knew Claire was probably a woman used to front seats and so was just doing what was natural, but this was too much.

Claire! Come here. I want to show you something. Claire had the door open and was about to toss her huge straw tote onto the seat (of course it matched her hat perfectly) but she stopped, flung the bag over her shoulder, and walked toward her, annoyed by the interruption. Althea was thrilled that Claire came when she clearly didn't want to because it meant she still had some kind of authority over her, at least when Ollie wasn't nearby.

But Althea didn't exactly have a plan. What was she going to show her? The cruddy green plastic sand buckets? The faded orange towels from Jonathan Adler? Claire was getting closer.

Then Althea noticed Claire's gold Hermès sandals with the *H*s on them and slammed the trunk shut.

Oui? What is it that is so interesting? Althea knew she had to make it quick. Ollie was still in the house, probably putting on sunscreen because he hated to do it at the beach, but he would be out soon.

See this? Althea bent down to touch the license plate and traced the letters with her fingers. It had been Oliver's idea. She used to think it was corny, but now it was like the sweater your mother insisted you bring on a cold day: in the end, you needed it.

A license plate? But all cars have them, Althea. That is not so unusual.

But read what it says.

C-I-A-O. Yes, Italian. For "hello." Or "goodbye." Claire did not sound impressed. Althea knew Claire thought it was almost as provincial as *B-O-N-J-R.*

Well, yes. But that's not it. It stands for Clem, Althea, and Oliver, with the I thrown in to make it a word. Althea stood and looked smugly at Claire; her car's sad little license plate was just a jumble of letters and numbers. Claire returned the look with nothing but derision.

We do not have these vanity plates, as you call them, in France. Plates there have to do with the government. I suppose we also think that things having to do with family are private. Claire walked back over to the front seat and got in.

They were going to Georgica Beach, one of the most popular and exclusive beaches. You had to have a pass, a sticker you put in your car's left rear window, to park there, and only so many permits were available. Many people who went there were just taking a day off from their clubs, going where they could read their iPads or gossip about other members without fear of reproach, and the rest were hoping to get into those clubs or were telling themselves that they didn't need them when Georgica was just as good. It was South of the Highway, the equivalent of upper Park or Fifth Avenue in the city. The sand was smooth, there was no snack bar, and the restrooms were as tasteful as bathhouses.

Before taking them to the beach, Oliver swung by the club. You couldn't get that close — it was gated — but you could circle the golf course and see the clubhouse gleaming in the background like some kind of Brigadoon. It was on the ocean; the green and white flags that flew from its roof beckoned like a receding tide.

To Althea, the club was a sort of parallel universe; it represented all the things she might have had if she hadn't been sick, things she had long ago given up on: beautiful friends with whom she could lob witty quips back and forth like tennis balls; couples she and Oliver would have dinners on the terrace with, drinking expensive wine or planter's punches (yes, she would be able to drink, even a lot, sometimes). Clem playing golf and swimming with the children of other club members; the three of them building beach bonfires with these children and their families or grilling at home with them or even traveling to other clubs (Lyford, Hobe Sound, Round Hill) with them. But she knew that even though she had given up wanting all of these things (or had never wanted them in the first place), Oliver hadn't. So whenever they went by the club, she couldn't help but think he was allowing himself the luxury of nursing one last hope.

And here you have it, Claire. The club. Home of the best lobster roll on the East End. Best golf course. The best —

The best lobster roll? You make it sound like a seafood stand, no? It is a very exclusive club, from what I know.

If a stand sells eighteen-dollar hot dogs, then I suppose it is a kind of stand. You do order lunch standing up.

Do not tease me. I have been there.

Of course you have, Althea thought. *When?* she asked.

With Georges. My cousin. It was just once. He was staying with a member and they invited me. I was the only woman wearing black. I'm sure I won't be asked to go again. Claire laughed. *But maybe if you join, you can bring me. Why do you not do this? Join?* Althea wanted to hit her. But she was also curious to see what Oliver would do. He hesitated. Reached for the radio. Fiddled.

They don't take my kind, Claire. I'm a merchant. That's all he said, and he spoke in such a tone it was hard to tell if he was kidding or not. But she seemed to believe him and looked like she felt bad for having asked the question. Surely she didn't understand enough about the American class system to know that Oliver's family money would have made him eligible for any club. Now she thought they saw him as the poor shop guy, selling sunglasses for a living. Forced to bring his own umbrella to the beach.

She wanted to laugh at Claire for believing this. And at the same time, she wanted to kiss Oliver, thank him. For even after the goodbye of the night before, goodbye to sex with her, he was still right there with her. He was keeping the secret of why things were the way they were. That secret was their intimacy, and as long as he didn't give it up, she would not lose him.

When they arrived at Georgica, it was still too early in the day to be crowded. Claire got out of the car, walked right over to the edge of the parking lot, and put her Hermès sandals in her straw bag. Claire either didn't know that people just kicked theirs off in the first pile of sand by the parking lot and left them unattended or really thought that someone (who had enough money to come to East Hampton) would steal her used shoes. In any case, Claire was not at all concerned about unloading the car. She took off to find a spot for them to settle.

Oliver shouldered the totes — with the towels, bottled water, sandwiches, and raspberry squares — and the four beach chairs. Althea took the umbrellas and the sand toys. This was the first time she had ever carried them. Clem followed behind, barely looking up from *Moby-Dick*. As far as Althea could tell, Oliver had yet to crack his. The place Claire had chosen for them was a bit too close to the water, but Althea didn't say anything. She didn't want Ollie to think she was picking a fight.

Claire stretched her arms to the sky like some kind of yoga salutation and then took off her white linen shift and put it in the straw bag, revealing a navy-blue bikini. There were the boobs and the belly again, and they seemed even bigger than yesterday, but Althea told herself maybe Claire was just getting on her nerves and it was merely a mirage. Still, she looked hot. Sexy. Jesus, life was unfair. Her husband found her repellent in lingerie, and most of the men on this beach would definitely fuck Claire in her unremarkable bikini with her stomach hanging out.

Claire fished around until she found a pack of Marlboro Reds, lit one, and inhaled it in a way that made smoking look sexy, not trashy. Clem folded down the corner of the page in her book and dug in the tote bag for a headband she had brought to keep her hair off her face. (How had she remembered to do this? Wasn't this something mothers did?) Althea dreaded having to put sunscreen on Clem. There was still a rawness between them from the night before, and besides, it was just so much work. But Clem was wearing a camo-print bikini and no cover-up or hat, and Althea knew that even though it was cloudy, you were still supposed to put it on.

Just when they were finally almost set up, a huge wave sprayed them. Claire had set her bag down close to the water to straighten her towel, and the whole thing got soaked.

Mon dieu. *My book is drenched. I can't just sit here with nothing to read.*

Then go home, Althea thought.

Why don't we take a beach walk? Ollie suggested. *I have to say, I would rather walk than sit any day. Althea? Clem? Join us?*

She was not big on beach walks, especially since Ollie was the type to make everything into a workout. Besides, if she didn't go, she would get a respite from Claire.

Thanks, but I'll stay here.

Clem?

I want to swim. Will you swim with me, Lune? Not this again. But this time would be different. They wouldn't be in a pool; they'd be in the ocean. And you couldn't really talk in the ocean.

Sure.

Okay, Oliver said. *See you in a bit.*

Just seeing them head off down the beach, watching their backs recede, made her realize that letting them leave together had been a mistake. It was the dishtowels all over again. Claire's pale shoulder blades jutted out just above the top tie of her bikini, and Ollie's white linen oxford rippled off his back like a flag. She had bought him that shirt for his birthday, and she had an urge to call out and remind him of this. Their bodies weren't touching, but they were close enough to each other to easily hold hands if they wanted to. Their heads were down, looking at the sand, and they were talking. About what? Spectacle? Her plans for the rest of the summer? How cold the water was as it ran over their feet? Anyone they passed would think they were a couple.

All of a sudden, she was jealous in the most visceral way. She would have wept over coffee to a best friend if she'd had one. She would have written pages and pages about it in a journal if she ever did such a thing. Instead, she imagined taking photos of Claire decapitated, her bloody torso floating out to sea. She glanced down and began clawing at her wrists. The pain grounded her.

She looked back to where they had been walking and realized she couldn't see them anymore. She felt sick all over again. She was about to dig through Claire's straw tote and throw her fucking ziplock bag of cherries into the ocean, but then she spotted Clem on the edge of the water, looking for sea glass. She had one of the buckets and was swinging it as she walked. She ran after her.

What'd ya get, Clem?

A couple of brown pieces, one green.

Is that good?

Green are the best. Then clear. The brown ones are kind of like brown M and M's — they're still M and M's, they taste the same as the other ones, but they're ugly, so you only eat them as a last resort. I keep some just to make the green ones look better.

Oh. I see, she said, though she didn't really. When she was little, a piece of sea glass was a piece of sea glass. The point was that it was rare among the shells, smooth in your hand.

What do you like about sea glass? Clem had been collecting it for years, and this was the first time she had asked her. She knew Clem would have a more complicated reason than she had had when she was a child.

It reminds me of cufflinks. Daddy's cufflinks.

Huh? Wouldn't it be pretty hard to get them through the holes?

Actually, that's not really it.

What, then?

I'd rather not say.

Oh. I understand. Though she didn't. *Well, what do you do with the glass?*

I sort it.

And then?

I look at it. I sort it. I don't know. What are you supposed to do with a collection?

I guess whatever you want. How many do you have?

About two hundred pieces.

How could she not have noticed Clem had amassed such a huge amount? Where did she keep it all? Did Oliver know? *How many are you going for?*

I don't know. I guess I'll be done when I'm done.

Althea was now almost desperate to know what it was about the sea glass that fascinated Clem. Maybe nothing that interesting after all. But she didn't believe obsessions ever grew from nothing that interesting.

She joined Clem in looking for glass, digging in the wet sand with her fingers, and she was practically ecstatic when she found one. Unfortunately, it was brown. But she was so happy to be in on the game, she didn't care.

Clem, look! I got one.

Thanks, Lune, Clem said. She took the sea glass in her hand, walked to the ocean, and rinsed off the sand, but she did not add it to the bucket.

Althea pretended not to notice and said:

Want to go swimming?

When Ollie and Claire came back, forty-five minutes later, she and Clem were lying down, drying themselves. The sun had come out from behind the clouds and it was getting hot. But Ollie and Claire were wet. She could see Claire's erect nipples through her suit. Ollie had his shirt tied around his waist; his canary-yellow shorts were soaked, and water still ran down the hair on his legs.

How was the walk? she said, attempting to sound casual, like she hadn't been checking her watch every five minutes and trying to pick them out of all the other couples now strolling on the beach.

Perfect, Claire said. *It was all of a sudden very hot so we went for a swim.*

We ran into Sasha, Oliver said. Not: *You should have come.* Sasha was a Tides mother who always called for playdates; Clem didn't like her daughter, so their nanny had to say no, but Sasha never gave up. *She said she would love to get together with us*, Oliver went on.

The woman was relentless. Or just stupid. But what Althea really wanted to ask was, *How did you introduce the young woman in the navy-blue bikini with the enormous breasts beach-walking with you? "She works for me"?* Instead she said:

Sorry I missed her. We had a blast here, though.

Clem opened her eyes.

Yes, Daddy, but it would have been more fun if you had been here.

Did she mean "It would have been more fun if you hadn't left"? Althea wasn't sure.

Well, I'm back. Another swim?

Sure, Clem said.

I'm in too, Althea added, even though she didn't really want to swim. But she was determined to grab Ollie's hand under the water. See if he would let her. Or at least brush her leg against his. He couldn't refuse that, could he? And off they went. Claire sat down on her towel but didn't bother to dry herself, as if wanting an imprint of her recent swim with Oliver on her body. Althea turned back and saw her watching as the three of them walked into the surf. Althea wasn't sure, but she could have sworn Claire glared at them.

THAT NIGHT WAS impossible. Even though Claire went to Southampton by herself to see a French film and Oliver grilled burgers bloody raw the way she liked, she still was completely consumed by Claire and Oliver's beach walk. Oliver had stuck close to Clem the whole time they were in the ocean and hadn't touched Althea once. She knew it must have been different with Claire. Did they hold hands? Or maybe brush fingers? Did Claire trip and grab Ollie's shoulder for balance? Had he noticed her erect nipples? She was still thinking about them; Ollie must be too.

She couldn't read before bed, she was so undone by the *promenade*, so she had listened to the water run as Oliver took his shower. She imagined him soaping his body, his face, scrubbing shampoo in his hair, thinking about his day with Claire. She was tempted to go in, try one more time, distract him, but she knew there was always the chance he might rebuff her again and she would just make herself feel worse. Even though he was right there, just feet away, she missed him like he had died.

Oliver finally emerged from the bathroom with his hair slicked back, dressed in pressed pajamas. They were the ones she had worn when she had been sick that year. She expected him to walk over to their bed, flip back the sheets on his side, and read before turning out the light. Instead, he said:

I'm going to run downstairs.

How come? Althea hoped the question sounded casual, not desperate and panicky.

Lydia didn't leave a drinking glass in the bathroom.

Cup your fucking hands, Althea wanted to say. But instead, she said:

Can you grab me some Pellegrino when you're down there? Althea hoped this would ensure Oliver really did go to the kitchen. And, more important, that he came back.

Oliver nodded, but he was already halfway out the door.

She waited ten minutes for him, then she turned out all the lights, put on her sleep mask, and put in her earplugs. She knew Claire must have just gotten back from her film and had probably ambushed Ollie in the kitchen, wanting to discuss it. But still, after the dishtowels and the beach walk, everything Claire did with Ollie made her crazy. As she lay there in bed, she began to obsess about the *Crepuscule* flag belt, the diamond sand necklace, the fucking ice cream maker. It was all too much. Claire had to go.

Oliver did indeed come back to their bedroom after about twenty minutes, and with a glass for the bathroom and a bottle of Pellegrino, but Althea still didn't sleep. She had made her mind up about Claire and spent the night ruminating on a maniacal loop about how she would *dispose* of her. She knew she couldn't just say, It isn't working out, like Claire was a girlfriend she was trying to let down gently. What reason could she give? Her work on the loft had been excellent and they hadn't even really gotten going on Lily Pond. My husband thinks you're hot? My daughter thinks you're cool? I'm an insecure mess? She would have to come up with something credible and less pathetic.

But then she reminded herself this was her house; she was in charge. Claire was little more than a service provider. She didn't owe her any explanations. She could just *Althea it*, as Ollie said, pretend she was just being flaky about the whole thing, backing out of the deal because she felt like it.

But what if Oliver stood up for Claire and insisted she stay? What if Claire refused to leave? What if Althea disappointed Clem again by not redoing her room?

But every time she was about to tell herself that it would be easier not to make a fuss and just keep Claire on, she paused, and that horrible feeling in her stomach came back. The only thing that would make it go away was watching Claire shove her enormous Tumi suitcase in her Mini and drive back to the city.

She finally got out of bed at six in the morning, moving as quietly as she could so as not to wake Oliver. She grabbed a pair of yoga pants that were frayed at the bottom. She looked through her stack of vintage T-shirts and then turned toward Oliver's half of the closet and saw the white linen shirt he had worn the previous day lying on the floor. (Oliver never managed to get things into the hamper.) There was still sand on it, and it looked rumpled-dirty, not rumpled-bohemian, but Althea picked it up and put it on anyway. She was his wife. She had the right to wear his clothes. She went to the kitchen to wait.

By the time Clem came down, around seven, Althea was on her fourth cup of coffee, trying to read the *East Hampton Star.* As always, she avoided the police blotter because she had been in it so many times during manic episodes. She had read the first page over and over without really comprehending it and had picked her nails clean of polish.

Hey, Lune. What are you doing up so early? I was expecting Daddy.

Who? Oh, yeah, that guy who lives here.

When Clem didn't so much as smile, she realized her mistake. She had no right to joke about Ollie to Clem. Clem could laugh at him, but Althea had long since lost the right to conspire.

She was a wreck. She knew Claire would probably be

down in about an hour. Althea wasn't sure she could wait that long.

No breakfast? Clem asked.

No, I'm about to throw up, Althea thought. But she said, *Not yet. I hoped you might make me some. I'm getting arthritic in my old age.*

You're only thirty-eight.

Bad genes, I guess.

Okay. But I only do Lucky Charms or toast.

Toast, please. Clem went to the toaster. Put it on high. They both liked it burned and with butter, and that day they ate it standing at the island.

An hour later, Claire finally came down in a lace V-neck cotton nightgown that showed off her cleavage. Althea imagined you could stick an airmail letter between her breasts and it would stay there. Her hair was tangled and down; her eyes were blinking furiously to adjust to the sunlight in the kitchen. Claire looked like she was just taking a break, stretching her legs, before going back to bed.

She walked over to the cabinet where the Willows kept their mugs without even saying hello, as if this were some kind of summer share and she had paid for the right to be there. She poured herself some coffee and drank it black.

That toast looks good, Claire said, eyeing the slice Althea had left untouched on her plate.

There's some bread in the fridge and the toaster's over there, she replied.

Oh, I never eat breakfast.

Of course not. How was the movie?

Good. Or I think it might have been. I fell asleep. The walk yesterday, it must be.

Three sips of coffee and Claire was awake and able to make Althea feel insecure.

That is Oliver's shirt from yesterday, no? You know, Althea, I really admire the fact that you don't care how you look.

If Althea had ever doubted her decision to give Claire the boot, she certainly didn't now. *I like to be comfortable.*

Of course. It was a compliment.

No, it wasn't. You think I'm a slob.

I didn't say that.

That's what I heard.

Bien. Have it your way. I just meant that you have a body that is almost good. Why cover it up with your husband's filthy shirts and those workout pants? Especially when you have money.

Clem stood there, silent but fascinated. Althea knew it was probably the first time she had seen two grown women fight.

Actually, the pants are from RLX. They cost three hundred dollars.

So you waste money too.

Claire, let's move on. I have something I want to talk to you about. She was glad that Claire had pissed her off. It would make firing her easier.

Bien. What is it? Claire sipped her coffee, checked her pedicure, and took the paper from where it sat on the island.

We won't need your services anymore.

What? Claire looked at Althea like she was kidding. *I don't understand.*

We don't need you going forward. For the project.

And why is that? Claire still seemed amused, like Althea had gotten it all wrong.

I'm going to do it myself. Althea was getting ahead of herself here, but she figured it couldn't be that hard.

Althea, chérie, *it is more difficult than it looks. I am sure you wouldn't want it not to turn out the way you want it.* Claire touched her shoulder like she was a child.

I'm not saying it won't be a challenge. I just want to give it a try. With Clem. But don't worry. I'll pay you anyway. It's only fair.

I don't care about the money, Althea. Didn't Oliver tell you? I'm actually doing this for free.

But I gave him money to pay you . . . a lot . . .

I told him to donate it to his charity.

Why are you doing this, Claire? Surely you could earn a lot of money elsewhere.

Althea . . . how should I say this . . . it is delicate . . . Ollie is a good friend, and I've watched him go through so much. So many troubles, especially this year. I wanted to help, but I didn't know how. And when this came up . . . I thought it might be a way for him to not have to worry.

Ollie's troubles? What was Claire talking about? Something at the office? *Especially this year . . .* Of course; she meant *her* troubles. And *Ollie?* Althea had thought she was the only one who called him this. But she wanted to know what Oliver had told her exactly.

And what are those? Ollie's troubles?

You know.

No, I really don't.

Well, I'll be frank. You. All that you have put him through over the years.

Especially when I fire his friend who is super-talented and comes to works for free . . .

What does Oliver think? Claire said.

He thinks your nipples are great, he really does. *It doesn't actually matter, Claire. What he thinks.*

Well, I'm going to ask him. And Althea watched as Claire ran up the stairs.

Did Daddy know you were going to do this? Clem asked.

It's our project, Clem.

I guess you're right. And Lune, I like you in Daddy's shirt.

SHE EXPECTED AT LEAST a little bit of crying from Claire, but she came down half an hour later in a teal cotton sundress and teal *vernis* flats, perfectly poised, with the Spectacle sunglasses secured on her face, the arms tucked into the sides of her chignon. Ollie followed just behind, carrying her suitcase and straw bag. His polo and shorts were pressed, and his hair was combed with a little bit of gel. He wasn't wearing shoes, and she thought, Thank God, he's not going to leave.

He didn't say anything, just glared at Althea.

Claire walked right up to Clem, now sitting on a stool at the kitchen island, watching the Weather Channel. Claire bent down, kissed Clem on the forehead, and said:

Au revoir, ma chérie. Claire lingered there, just a second, waiting for a response, but Clem gave her none. Claire straightened and strode over to the pantry. Althea wondered if she was grabbing a snack for the road. Claire threw the door open, made a big show of pushing things around on the shelf, reached in, and then turned back to them holding the ice cream maker.

Perfect, Althea thought. I won't have to schlep to the Ladies Village Improvement Society to donate it.

But instead of carrying it to the door, and just as Oliver said, *Here, let me help you* (why did he always have to be so fucking polite?), Claire hurled it at Althea, who ducked just in time to keep the goddamned thing from hitting her in the head. It went crashing to the floor. She looked at Clem, and they both had to work not to laugh. That was the beauty of Clem, Althea thought; stuff like this didn't faze her. She could see how absurd it was. Oliver went to Clem at once.

Easy, Claire! Althea, are you okay? He looked in her direction but made no move toward her. Claire did. She put her face right up in Althea's and said: *You're a crazy mess,* salope. *You ruin everything.* She took her straw bag from Oliver and walked out to her car.

Drive safely, Althea said in her most cheerful voice.

Oliver grabbed Althea by the upper arm and dragged her to the sunporch, leaving Clem in the kitchen.

Althea, what the fuck? How could you fire her?

I didn't want to work with her anymore.

I'm not going to ask why, but you didn't even run it by me first.

Since when do I have to run everything by you?

You're on heavy medication and your judgment is impaired.

Bair said I'm stable.

Claire works for me at Spectacle!

Which is where she should have stayed.

Althea, cut it out. Claire said she wanted to leave anyway. Said you were difficult.

I'm difficult? *She just threw an ice cream maker at my head.*

You blindsided her.

That was straight-up psycho behavior.

If you have to know, she's very fragile right now. She's pregnant.

Really? Who's the father?

She's not telling people.

She doesn't know?

No, she's just not telling people.

Poor Claire. She got knocked up.

Althea, stop it.

Well, is she in a relationship? Or did she do IVF?

No, and no. But cut it out. The real issue is, I want you to apologize to her.

I will not.

Yes, you will.

You can't make me.

Clearly, I can't. But I wish you would.

Don't hold your breath.

Althea, look. If that's how you want to act, I can't stop you. But I'm not going to just sit here. I'm going to the city. And not coming back for a while.

What? Why is this so important to you?

You totally humiliated her and embarrassed our family.

What about Clem? You can't just not see her for the rest of the summer. (Read: You can't just leave me alone with her.)

Send her to me on the weekends.

Like a package?

No, like a ten-year-old on the jitney.

But that will be disruptive to her. To me.

It will be fine. You'll see.

When are you leaving?

Now. I'm driving Claire into the city.

Oh.

Just then she remembered his bare feet. He must be bluffing. He noticed her looking.

I couldn't find my loafers. Have you seen them?

Behind the hamper.

Thanks.

They drove off in Claire's Mini. Before they left, Clem went out to say goodbye but Althea couldn't bear it. She watched from the window. Why didn't she just apologize? Because she knew she was right. Standing up for that was certainly worth something, even if the price was high. She and Ollie had never spent more than five nights apart except when she was in the hospital.

Once Claire and Ollie had left, she took her and Clem's plates to the sink, rinsed them, and put them in the dishwasher, a task she normally left for Coco. Clem went back to watching the Weather Channel.

Heat advisory in Miami, Clem said.

Clouds in East Hampton, she replied as she dried the counter by the sink.

Now she just had to figure out how to redo a damn house.

| | | | | | |

THAT NIGHT, she and Clem sat in Clem's room. She was still wearing Ollie's shirt, and Clem had on jean cutoffs like Althea's and a T-shirt that said PUT ME ON.

Lune, is Daddy really mad at us or is he just trying to make Claire feel better because we fired her?

First of all, he's not mad at you, he's mad at me. As for his leaving, Claire was acting kind of crazy, as you saw. Daddy probably didn't think it was safe for her to drive to the city.

But when is he coming back?

Soon.

Are you just saying that?

Clem, we have a lot to do before camp begins next week. We're going to start with painting your room. You need to pick colors. Any ones you want. We're also doing mine and the guest room.

Cool.

Do you have any idea what colors you want? You need something for the walls, ceiling, and trim. They don't all have to be different.

I want purple and silver.

But those are my favorite colors.

It's not like you can own colors, Lune.

I know, but I'm going to use them. Don't you want something different . . . like —

Orange, I know. No. White.

But your walls are already white.

Black, then.

Depressing.

How about cream with cream trim?

You don't want anything more interesting?

No. *That would be perfect.*

Okay, tomorrow we can go to the hardware store and pick out the paint, find a painter. It doesn't sound like we would need Claire for that.

CLEM AND ALTHEA drove into town to Village Hardware, right in the middle of Newtown Lane, Clem holding notes they had taken the night before, as if they might not remember the four colors they had chosen. They waded through the aisles, which were jammed with everything from irons to camouflage duct tape, and made it to the back of the store. There was a boy, about twenty-one, Althea guessed, standing by the paint display, fiddling with his phone.

Althea waited for him to finish what he was doing — texting, she supposed. His fingers were all over the screen. She wondered if he was chatting with a girl, making plans, or having an argument. The phone had a decal of a surfboard on the back of it. Finally, he noticed Clem and Althea standing there and reluctantly slipped the phone into the back pocket of his jeans.

Sorry, the boy said, but Althea thought it sounded like he was actually expecting *them* to apologize for interrupting *him.* He was wearing a faded blue T-shirt that hung out over his pants and had white paint stains on it. *Can I help you?*

Yes, um, we want to buy some paint, Althea said.

Sure. She waited for a follow-up question, but there was none.

It's for a house.

Usually is. Inside or out?

Some rooms. So inside, I guess.

Don't you have a decorator? Most people around here do.

Well, we did, but she went on a beach walk with my husband and threw an ice cream maker at my head. Althea might have said this if he were a woman about her age who would think she was kidding or maybe realize she was telling the truth but understand and laugh anyway. But Althea knew this would all go right over the boy's head and he would just think she was insane.

No, we don't. It's just a project my daughter and I are taking on. For fun.

Right.

She could tell by his tone he thought she was a total idiot. *So can we see some samples?*

We have a lot of them. Do you have any colors in mind?

Cream, Clem said.

And purple and silver. For the master and the guest bedrooms, she said.

He turned before she could finish her sentence, making it clear he didn't really care what color went with what room or, really, what rooms she was painting.

He tossed her some strips of paper that were in the color families she'd said she wanted. Then the boy said:

Listen, it's my lunch. Pick out some samples and then you can come back and order.

Thank you . . . um . . .

Dylan.

And he was off. But not before pausing to help a cute girl who was apparently having a hard time picking out scented candles. She had blond hair to her shoulders, still wet from the beach or maybe a postbeach shower, and her legs were glistening with lotion. Dylan brushed her arm repeatedly as he smelled the candles with her, giving his opinion on each, and finished by punching her number into his phone. Althea wondered if the girl had given him the right one, but Dylan was good-looking and the blonde was rolling up on her toes to meet his eyes; of course she had. The girl stopped at the register to buy a candle. Dylan waved at her as he left, and Althea envied them their first dinner, their first fuck, even their first fight.

COCO MADE CLEM and Althea squash soup and chicken breasts for dinner that night, and Althea felt a dark mood coming on. Not an all-out one — she wasn't the sort of person who threw *depression* around when she was just having a dip — but it was bad enough that she didn't really want to be alone. She missed Oliver.

She and Clem sat on her bed, leaning on the king-size down pillows, and spread out the color strips they had gotten. Clem circled the ones she wanted, then got a legal pad and wrote down the numbers and the names.

Althea watched Clem's hand grip the pencil so tightly that the blood drained out of her fingers as she pressed the words into the paper. Althea realized (she had never really studied it before) how sweet and earnest her writing was, each letter strong and crooked at the same time, like a child's teeth.

Althea was still not feeling up to picking her paint colors. She thought she just might let Clem do it. Picking more colors would take Clem at least another hour or so. How could Althea possibly do a whole house? Maybe she could just do these three rooms, or at least get them painted and then hire another decorator? That was fair, wasn't it?

The next morning, Althea felt worse. She was *in a bad space*, as some people called it, like a king about to be mated in a game of chess. It wasn't the Tombs, thank God, it wasn't worthy of a visit to Bair, but everything was heavy and gray and she just wanted to be alone. She would have to wait on the painting as well; she just couldn't face Dylan.

She called Oliver. It was eight thirty. He would have been at the office for twenty minutes.

This is Oliver.

Ollie.

What's up? Althea could tell he was reading the paper as he talked.

I'm just not feeling so great.

How not so great? Do you need to see Bair?

Well, no.

Spending time with Clem?

Yes.

So, what's the problem?

It's just I'm a bit down.

Althea, I'm not coming out because you are in a bad mood.

I didn't ask you to.

You did. Though not in so many words.

I just wanted to check in.

Thank you for letting me know, then. How's Clem?

Good. We've started on the house.

Really? Just the two of you?

Yes. Only a few things. But it's going.

That's terrific. Look, if it gets worse, call me.

Of course.

But I do think it's good for you and Clem to have some time alone. For you too.

Sure.

THE FOLLOWING WEEK, she dropped Clem at camp, and her black mood lifted. She didn't know if she felt relieved because her days were free again or because, like all her moods, it left because it wanted to. They talked to Oliver every night, assured him all was well, so much so that Clem told him she wanted to wait before going into the city to visit, which Althea took as a small victory.

She decided to walk to town and try again at the hardware store. She hadn't done anything remotely active for a while. It took a good twenty-five minutes to get there, but the exertion made her feel even better. When she opened the door, she didn't dare go to the back, just went up front to the register. There was a friendly-looking older man with the name HAL stitched on his shirt leaning on the counter reading the paper. He looked up at her and smiled, the kind of smile that said he really wanted to be useful and sell her something, or maybe that he was just glad she was there. The store was practically empty. Everyone was probably shopping for cover-ups or sitting by the pool. No one wanted to buy hammers when it was eighty degrees out.

Hello, Hal said. *Can I help you?* She liked how he said *Can*

I *help*, as if he knew she had other problems and was willing to listen. She almost said, My husband won't have sex with me anymore and decided to spend the summer in the city because I fired our decorator who was trying to sleep with him, and I'm not sure how to rectify the situation; what do you think I should do? Surely Hal, who was no doubt happily married, would take pity on her and offer some avuncular advice. But she saw the bins of nails on the wall behind him and remembered where she was. Jesus, Althea, she said to herself. Get it together. She handed him the color strips.

I'd like to buy some paint.

What are you painting?

She explained.

You can't just buy that amount of paint; we'll have to order it. A painter usually takes care of that for you. Do you have one?

No. I mean, I was hoping you might recommend someone.

Sure. For bigger jobs, most people go to Aboff's. But yours seems manageable. I know a good kid.

How old is he?

Twenty-one. He'll be a senior at New Paltz. But he's responsible. Shows up on time. Works hard. Doesn't chat, get in your business, the way people do out here . . .

Could I try him out? Maybe have him do a baseboard or something? Just to make sure he's good?

Well, that's not really how it works. You hire someone or you don't. If you want to know if they're good, you check references. At least three. And then maybe go see their past projects.

She never checked references, which made Ollie crazy. Her theory was that people weren't going to refer you to former employers who might say that they were dodgy, incompetent, or simply mediocre. So Althea relied on instinct. If the good kid mixed up the different shades of cream or got paint on Althea's wood floor, it wouldn't be a big deal. It wouldn't be a Claire situation. She could just tell him to go, no drama.

So, would you be able to set all this up for me? The painter? I'll give you my address and maybe he could even stop by tomorrow?

Hal laughed. *I'll get you his number. I just make recommendations.*

Oh, okay. She fought the urge to be mad at Hal, who she thought was holding out on her. Why couldn't anyone in this place be unequivocally helpful?

Sorry, what's his name?

Maze.

Maze?

Maze.

Oh.

He gave her the number.

She couldn't explain it, but just the idea of Maze, this boy she hadn't even met yet, made her happy. It was the first time she was hiring someone without running it by Oliver. On her way back home, she stopped at the Golden Pear and bought a cup of pineapple, which she was positive happy people ate.

By the time she went to call Maze that night, though, she was a wreck. If he said no, she would be completely humiliated. It would be a laundry-room-lingerie situation all over again. A Dylan-and-his-phone-refusing-to-wait-on-her-because-she-wasn't-young-and-cute-enough scenario. But she couldn't not call him. That would mean she was giving up. And why shouldn't Maze help her? It was an easy job. She would pay him well. It wasn't as if he could see what she looked like over the phone.

Althea was literally shaking when she dialed. She almost hung up so she could rehearse what she was going to say, but then she remembered her number would appear on Maze's caller ID, so she had no choice but to wait for him to pick up.

Hello? He answered on the fourth ring.

Maze? Should Althea have said *hello* back? She wasn't sure of telephone etiquette for his generation. But, really, who else would have answered his phone?

Yep. This is Maze. Can I help you? She had expected him to sound younger. His voice was as deep as Oliver's. But Oliver would never say *Yep*.

Hal gave me your number. I was looking for someone to paint my house. Well, not the whole thing, just three rooms. He told me you might be interested . . .

I'd be totally up for that. I've got nothing going on right now. Something I was working on got delayed. They can't decide on fabrics.

Oh. That must be annoying.

Not really. It's their house. They want to get it right. Althea had made her first mistake with Maze: Never criticize people you don't know to someone you don't know.

I just meant — nothing against them — that you must have blocked out time and everything, and now you have to scramble . . .

I never scramble. Even though Maze said this in an offhand way, not as a criticism of her, she still felt like a complete idiot. Second mistake: Never tell someone he scrambles.

I shouldn't have assumed you did. Scramble. I just do, and, well, I know a lot of people who do too, but clearly you aren't one of them. I mean, I can already tell . . . Just stop now. Talk about the job. Before he changes his mind.

So tell me about the job.

There are three rooms I want painted. The walls are in great condition so it's pretty straightforward. I've already picked out the colors, so there won't be a decorator involved bothering you. Just me. I won't be bothering you, I mean, just telling you what paint to order and being around in case you have questions. But I don't hover. I never hover. She waited for Maze to ask her what kind of work she did, maybe where she lived or even what her name was, but he didn't.

I can certainly do that.

What would you, I mean, what do you normally . . . I mean, I want to be fair. This was the first time Althea had tried to negotiate pay with someone, and clearly she would have been more comfortable asking Maze about the last time he had had sex. Luckily he interrupted her, managing to do it in a pleasant but professional tone.

It really depends. I have to do a walk-through and see the scope of the project first. I'll give you an estimate, and usually, if there aren't any big surprises, I come pretty close. I charge by the job, not by the hour. People say I'm fair, but if you think the price is too high, you are welcome to find someone else after the walk-through, no hard feelings.

Of course, Maze didn't know that Althea didn't care what he charged. She wouldn't know if it was high or low anyway, and she certainly wasn't going to check with anyone else. Who was she going to call besides Ollie? Her neighbor who hadn't talked to Althea since she had done something — something *beyond the pale*, as the neighbor said — when she had been in the Visions and that she didn't even remember?

That sounds more than reasonable, Maze. When can you come for the walk-through?

Whenever works. Althea didn't want to seem desperate, but she also didn't want him to change his mind.

How about tomorrow morning. Around nine? Was that pushing it? She added, *I get busy as the summer goes on.* She was planning to work. Especially now that she was putting the major house redo on hold. If only she could get inspired.

Fine by me.

Althea gave him the address. *And Maze? It's Althea.*

Got it.

See you tomorrow.

Right.

For the walk-through.

Yep.

You know where our house is?

Yep.

Okay. Well . . . thanks for agreeing to meet so quickly.

No problem.

Goodbye, then.

See ya.

She hit the end button on her cell phone. She hadn't wanted to hang up; she'd wanted to confirm their appointment one more time and also explain to Maze that she wasn't normally such an idiot.

She had no clue what to wear for their first meeting. She wanted to look cool, whatever that meant, but not like she had worked at it. Her goal was for Maze to see she was totally different from all of the society women he had surely worked for South of the Highway. Althea planned to explain that she really didn't have any friends and that she hated parties, because she was sure Maze was like that too. But then Althea decided to say nothing. He probably didn't care what she did in her free time. No matter what she wore, Maze was there to paint her house. That was all.

Still, Althea chose her clothes carefully, settling on a vintage white lace skirt and a denim oxford shirt. Bare feet. She pushed her long hair off her face with her purple sunglasses and put on just a touch of lipstick. At two minutes to nine, a silver truck slid into the driveway, spraying pebbles and coming just a bit too close to Ollie's Porsche as it parked. Maze. Althea hoped briefly that he would ding the door of the Porsche when he opened his. But, no, he'd left just enough space.

Maze got out. God, he was beautiful, was Althea's first thought. God, he was young, was her second one. Althea wiped her hands on her shirt, even though they were perfectly clean, and walked toward him.

Maze was tall, about six two, but he slouched a bit. His shoulders were broad but curved forward; his hands quickly found his pockets like he was cold. He had thick dark hair between curly and straight that Althea guessed stayed wet for hours after he showered. His eyes were such a dark brown, they absorbed rather than reflected light. There was more than a bit of stubble on his chin, which meant he was still young enough not to make shaving a priority. He probably got to it once in a while. He was wearing a faded green T-shirt that said GREEN in white block letters, baggy jeans (streaked with paint, of course), and tan work boots. Even though his T-shirt was as loose as a luffing sail, she could see his stomach was so toned it was concave.

He turned to look at her and squinted in the sun. She wondered if he hadn't worn sunglasses on purpose or if he had just forgotten them in the truck. Maybe she should pull a Claire and give Maze the pair Ollie always left in the front hall. She decided to see how things worked out.

Maze walked over to where she was standing, about ten feet from the truck, and stopped.

Hey, he said. *Hope I'm not late.*

No, you're perfect.

She realized after a moment that Maze was waiting. It was her move, her job to tell him what to do. Althea considered her options. Would a handshake be too formal? It was business, after all. Then she noticed his hands were covered with paint and she wasn't sure he would want her touching them. She decided on a small hug, which, it turned out, couldn't have been a worse idea. Althea leaned in and put her arms around his shoulders, and Maze's whole body stiffened. Jesus, this was awkward. At least she hadn't tried to kiss him on the cheek. But Maze was just a boy. What else was he going to do when a strange, middle-aged woman hugged him?

She released him like it was all *totally cool* and launched into the babble she was so good at.

I notice you're passionate about the environment. Passionate about the environment? Who says that?

Huh? Maze put his hand up to shield his eyes. His tone was encouraging, but Althea could tell he had no idea what she was talking about.

Your shirt. Green.

Oh, yeah. That. I almost went to Dartmouth. To swim.

Wow. Ivy League. What happened? Maze took his hand away from his eyes, began scratching his elbow.

The usual. Money. Althea was completely mortified. Of course it was money. And she'd made him admit his family didn't have any. But Maze was calmly picking at a loose thread of his T-shirt, like it was no big deal. Still, Althea felt the need to say:

I wanted to go to Stanford. My parents might have been able to afford it, but it turns out I was too stupid to get in.

New Paltz works for me.

It's a great school. Really, it is. I mean, it's not like students who go there don't get good jobs or go to graduate school when they finish. People just get too label-conscious, and if something's not an Ivy, well, it's not on their radar. Althea wished she would just shut up. *What's your major?*

Engineering.

Really? That's impressive. I mean, I don't even really know what engineering entails. I mean, I know there's building involved, but that's about it. Just stop now, Althea. Ask a simple question before he gets in his truck and drives away. *I'm an English person.*

That's my minor. Not officially, but I take lots of courses.

Wow. What do you like to read?

All sorts of stuff.

Like?

Well, right now, I'm really into David Foster Wallace.

Althea had never read him and had nothing intelligent to say about his work. *He's brilliant.*

Totally.

She was trying to think of something else to talk about when Maze surprised her with:

I also try to write.

Really? What kinds of things?

I don't know. Stuff. Maze looked down and began picking his cuticles.

Do you ever show it to people?

Nah. It's basically garbage so far.

You're probably just being hard on yourself.

I doubt it. I pretty much know what works and what doesn't. But anyway . . . Maze glanced at the drop cloths in the back of this truck. He suddenly seemed impatient, like she had been wasting his time. And here she'd thought he had been enjoying their conversation, opening up a bit.

Let me show you the house.

THE WALK-THROUGH WENT WELL, and Maze started two days later, as soon as the paint came in and the Willows' caretaker, Frank, had removed all the furniture from the guest room. She spotted a pink coral button from one of Claire's Liberty blouses on the floor where the nightstand had been. She felt like doing something violent to it, but what were the options? Flush it down the toilet? Smash it with a hammer? Both seemed kind of childish and not even that rewarding, but she still hated Claire that much. Althea left the button sitting there, knowing that when Lydia cleaned the room, she would find it and put it in the sewing kit. Since Althea didn't even know where the sewing kit was, she would never have to see it again.

Once again, Maze arrived early. This time, he walked right up to the house. She was just opening the door and almost tripped over him. Or into him. It was hard not to hug him, their bodies were so close, but Althea knew from before not to, so she just shook his hand.

Maze was wearing the same work boots and jeans, still paint-spattered, but he had on a pale blue T-shirt that was clean, and his face and hands were too. He had shaved, and there was a little nick on his chin that was still just a bit wet with blood. She couldn't remember the last time Oliver had cut himself shaving. Maze reached up and touched the cut, checking to see if it was still there (of course it was), and then wiped his fingers on his shirt. She wondered if Maze noticed she was looking at it. Would he wash the shirt later, know how to get out the stain? Or maybe his mother still did his laundry? His hair was still wet, and she wondered if it smelled like salt water from an early-morning swim at the beach or like some all-purpose soap, Dove or something.

Hey, he said.

She had told him to call her Althea, but he was probably shy about it since she was so *old.* Maze touched his face again. Althea wanted to get him a Band-Aid. She knew there were some in Clem's room, but they were either neon or had Hello Kitty! on them. She decided the best thing would be to just ignore it.

Hey, Maze, she said. Just saying his name gave her a head rush, like she had broken new ground in their relationship.

I'll just get my stuff from the truck.

She didn't want him to start work yet. She had promised she

wouldn't hover over him, and she wouldn't, really. But she'd stayed up almost all night trying to figure out something special to do for Maze on his first day on the job, before he actually started. Then she'd remembered that the boys she had dated in college were always hungry. She would feed him. Coco always kept the kitchen stocked with fresh pastries from Mary's Marvelous for Clem and Oliver. Althea never ate them.

Hold on. I have breakfast inside. Fresh OJ, coffee, pastries . . .

Thanks, but I'm good.

But there's everything. Cinnamon rolls, muffins . . .

Really, it's okay. I ate already. Althea imagined him standing at the kitchen counter eating a bowl of cereal, barely enough milk to cover the flakes. No napkin; juice straight out of the carton. But he was six two. A swimmer. Surely there was always room for more.

I have high ceilings, remember? You'll need the energy. She was not going to beg, but she was coming close.

Maze seemed to understand that this was no longer about food.

Right. In that case, I'd love some.

SHE LED HIM through the screen door to the kitchen. Fresh OJ in a glass pitcher, a woven tray holding about five different kinds of baked goods (all warm), Spode dessert plates, ironed linen napkins, a large silver pot of coffee, Tiffany mugs, and French vanilla creamer took up the entire kitchen island.

Maze grabbed two enormous carrot muffins with cream-cheese frosting, two maple scones, and a huge tumbler of OJ.

He scarfed the pastries down using a napkin, no plate. Maze's mouth was continuously full for about five minutes. There was silence except for the sound of his chewing, which didn't seem to bother him. When he was finally done eating, he downed the juice in about three gulps and wiped his mouth with the back of his hand. Finally he turned to her — she had been sitting there, just watching him — and said:

This is completely awesome. Thank you.

You're completely welcome. How about some coffee?

Um, I don't drink coffee. I should really get started. He disappeared through the door, out to his truck.

When Maze came back, she followed him up to the guest room. She was most definitely hovering. She asked if he needed help, but Maze wouldn't let her so much as touch anything. He stacked the drop cloths in the middle of the floor and was about to spread them out when he paused and strode over to the baseboard. Something had caught his attention, and he bent down to look. There was the hairline crack that Althea started to tell Maze she already knew about. But that wasn't it.

You lost a button, Maze said, picking it up. Christ. Claire's button. Althea should have smashed it after all. Maze reached out his hand to give it to her.

It's not mine, Althea said, backing away.

Oh. Do you know whose it might be?

Of course not. Why would I?

Well, do you want it? Maze was shaking Claire's button like a die in his open palm. *Mind if I keep it?*

If you want to, of course not. Really, what could she say?

Maze shoved the button into the front pocket of his jeans.

She wished she had taken Claire's fucking button. Claire

didn't even know Maze and somehow she'd managed to get into his pants.

What are you going to do with it?

Dunno. Never know when a button might come in handy. I keep stray ones in a jar on my desk.

And then . . . ?

I sew them on my shirts . . . or whatever.

You sew?

Yep.

I don't believe you.

Yeah. Good skill to have.

Impressive.

Not really. It's not hard. You can make all kinds of stuff if you can sew.

Like what?

Well, my wallet. Maze pulled a white canvas square from his back pocket and handed it to Althea.

Um, no offense, but were you working off some kind of pattern or was it a let's-see-what-happens situation?

That's probably evident. I made it out of a piece of sail.

Oh. Cool.

So now she knew that Maze loved to write and that he had sewn his own wallet out of a sail. She felt like it was a challenge to get as many details out of him as she could before he inevitably shut her down. She continued.

Do you want something else to eat?

Since twenty minutes ago? Nah.

How's the writing? Are you doing any this summer?

I should really start working.

There's no rush, Maze.

I'm sure you're busy too.

I just want you to feel comfortable here, working for me.

I'm pretty much never uncomfortable.

Well, will you let me know if you are?

Not going to happen.

I just meant if there's anything I could do to improve your work environment. (Wow, seriously? Althea thought.)

IT TOOK MAZE four days to finish painting the guest room. When Clem was at camp, Althea spent the time in her office trying to get started on a new project. She usually developed a concept first and then figured out how she would concretize it on film. She told herself she wasn't stuck, just tunneling deeper than usual. She doodled in her notebook, paced around her room, flipped through some magazines, but nothing came to her. Then Althea realized she wasn't thinking about photography. She was thinking about Maze.

The day he completed the guest room, while Clem ate dinner with Coco, Althea went and sat by herself in the empty space. The walls were light silver. Actually, *silver* was generous — even she had to admit, if only to herself, that they really looked gray. But gray was better than before. They had been a cobalt blue, and blue was more a Claire color. Silver was hers. She wondered what Maze thought of it. Maze, who had spent all those hours with those brushes and cans, wiping the paint on his jeans, getting it under his fingernails. She knew by now that he wouldn't have told her the truth if she'd asked him.

What *had* he been thinking about? Besides doing a good

job (she knew he was thinking this), what else? Had he noticed her bare feet that morning when she opened the door, toes polished silver as a nod to the job? Maze probably had a girlfriend and was thinking about her. Listening to the lyrics of the songs on the radio, thinking about her. But Maze didn't seem that romantic. He was probably pondering what he was going to do after work. Surf? Bike? Watch TV? Eat? Of course. Eat.

She crawled over to the pile of drop cloths in the middle of the room. She lay down and looked up at the ceiling like she was outside on the grass and it was the nighttime sky. She felt something hard against her head. She sat up and felt for it. It was Maze's wallet. She ran her fingers over it and imagined him cutting the pieces of sail, sewing them together. Why did he do this? Where did he ever get the idea? There was something so sweet about it, she just wanted to hold it against her chest. It was like a project Clem might have done in school and brought home to give her as a present. But Maze had made the wallet for himself and had put his twenty-one-year-old-boy things inside.

There wasn't much in it. As she'd guessed, Maze would never carry things he couldn't use. In his wallet, he kept thirteen dollars. (Three ones and a ten.) His driver's license — a picture of Maze with longer hair, white T-shirt; date of birth: March 8, 1993. The card slots were a little too tight and she had to yank the rest of the items out. There was a CVS card, and it touched her to think how organized Maze was, how he must care about the money he might save. Althea could never bring herself to bother with the hassle of the paperwork involved in getting one, and the nice woman who rang her up usually gave her the discount anyway. There was his New Paltz ID, a debit card from Chase Bank (how much was in there, she wondered, given the thirteen dollars in the wallet?). A water-safety instructor certification. Then a piece of notebook paper, so worn she was afraid she would rip it when she opened it.

There are very few innocent sentences in writing. — David Foster Wallace

The handwriting was cramped and slanted to the left, but it was legible. It had been written in a black ballpoint, so none of the words had smeared. They were as immutable as dried paint. She knew the quote was something he had copied from Wallace, but Althea felt like it was the closest she had come to knowing what he really thought about. And it was about being deceptive. No; more like disingenuous. That was Maze.

She decided to call him.

He answered on the fifth ring, right before it went to voicemail. She knew the formula; Oliver frequently didn't pick up right away.

Yeah? He sounded half asleep. She wondered if he often went home to nap after finishing work. He must be tired. She couldn't help thinking about him answering the phone in his bed. Well, she assumed he was in bed, but then she remembered boys his age could fall asleep anywhere.

Maze, it's Althea. You left your wallet. I thought you might need it before tomorrow.

Oh. That's okay.

Are you sure?

Yep. He yawned and Althea could almost see him pushing his hair back from his face.

Well, don't you need it to drive tomorrow? I mean, it's always a good idea to have your license. I was stopped once without mine and got a huge ticket.

I'll risk it. But thanks.

Althea was not willing to give up.

I'm happy to bring it to you, she said.

Seriously, not necessary.

It's really not a problem. Where do you live?

It's kind of far.

Where? She imagined sitting on his bed. Looking at his posters. He must have posters on his walls, no?

Springs.

That's not far, Maze, seriously.

I'll get it in the morning. But thanks anyway. Before Althea could think of another argument for going over there, he hung up.

She held his wallet in her hand, torn between throwing it at the wall and rubbing the sailcloth across her cheek. She thought about the quote inside. *There are very few innocent sentences in writing.* She told herself that at least she shared one of his secrets now. The problem, of course, was that Maze didn't know it.

ALTHEA IGNORED MAZE the rest of the week. She was furious at him for not wanting her to come over and at herself for being upset about it. She got even more angry when he didn't notice or didn't care about her change in demeanor. He asked her for what little direction he needed and then just kept painting. He didn't even bother to thank her for finding his wallet. This more than anything pissed Althea off until she realized he hadn't lost it; he'd just left it with his stuff. Althea was irritable with Clem, so much so that she started having Frank, the caretaker, drive Clem to and from camp. The girl seemed relieved to go visit Oliver that weekend.

By the beginning of the next week, Althea was exhausted. She wanted to seem easygoing, but her anger had gained so much momentum that she didn't know how to make such an abrupt switch. So she moped. This seemed like a good compromise. She asked Maze how things were going but in a tone that dragged and begged him to ask her what was wrong. Of course he didn't. Which made her mope even more. It was after Althea had almost cried in front of him that she finally got herself together and snapped out of it. She told herself all of the madness was just because she missed Oliver. That had to be it.

Maze was painting the ceiling in the master. After that, he had only Clem's room left. Probably about a week in all.

But then there was the sticker.

She was sitting by the pool reading *Infinite Jest*. She had been carrying the tome around with her for days, sometimes even leaving it in the room where Maze was working or on the landing of the stairs, coming back to get it later. It had been her last effort to get Maze to engage in some kind of non-work-related conversation, which of course he hadn't. She finally gave up on the *Infinite Jest* game and decided to actually read it. She was almost an hour into the book, on page 7, when she looked up and saw him standing over her. Maze put his hand on the top of her deck chair, a way of tapping her on the shoulder without actually touching her. He was sweating through his shirt, and she could see small breakouts at his hairline and under his chin. She knew he would stop getting them in a year or so, but he probably didn't think that far ahead yet. Maybe he would have if he hadn't had so much to worry about right now. The next job after hers, the loans at New Paltz.

Whatever Maze's future plans were, at the moment, standing next to her deck chair in his jeans and T-shirt, he looked uncomfortably hot. She wanted to tell him to change into one of Ollie's bathing suits and take a swim. But she knew he would refuse, and then she would feel like an idiot for asking, and they would be right back where they'd started. So she just tilted her head up at him with a benign smile like he was a waiter there to take her drink order.

There's a sticker on the ceiling. Should I scrape it off or do you want me to try to peel it off and keep it intact? If it were anyone but Maze, she might have thought he was making an excuse to talk to her. *Should I peel off or scrape off your sticker?* It sounded absurd. But Maze was just being himself. Checking, being thorough. A boy who didn't throw away stray buttons.

What she didn't yet realize was that Maze was also a boy who understood that a sticker doesn't just end up on a ceiling.

I'm sorry. What did you say?

There's this sticker. On the ceiling. And . . .

Oh. That.

The sticker was a yellow smiley face the size of a silver dollar that Ollie had stuck up there during a long summer of the Tombs. Althea loved kitsch whether she was well or sick. Of course Oliver never left Althea in East Hampton by herself overnight when she was ill, but when he was at the beach or at the pool with Clem, and Althea was in bed all day, the sticker reminded her she was still part of them, that they loved her. And when she was well, and Ollie was sleeping in the city, Althea would look at Mr. Smiley and love the fact that she had the kind of husband who would put a sticker on top of an expensive paint job just to cheer her up.

It's right above where the bed was.

Above the bed. Of course.

But back then, there were days when she and Oliver could joke about Mr. Smiley. One night, during a summer so good that Althea was able to read and slept in a black camisole, albeit with waffle pajama pants, he had gone to a barbecue. Ollie had come back happy-drunk from too much beer and had flirted with her.

You know, Thea, Smiley is really a high-tech camera I installed to make sure no one sleeps on my side of the bed when I'm in the city.

Few things are more innocent than sleeping, you know, Althea replied, not believing Oliver took an interest.

Maybe. Then it's the waking up that I'm worried about.

If I want to take a lover, you're going to need more than Smiley here to stop me.

Smiley has many friends. In many places. Oliver sounded serious all of a sudden.

So do I, love.

I don't think so. You hate people.

Most, yes. All, no. But best for you never to leave. That's really your only option.

Oliver rolled toward her and bit her shoulder. She felt a little tickle between her legs. While Althea still responded to him on the meds, she rarely got a release, so they hardly tried anymore. But that night, he'd slid his hand between her legs, started stroking her. He pulled off her top, kissed the space between her breasts, then began rolling his tongue around one of her nipples.

If I want to take a lover . . . But of course she never had. For better or worse. Since the night Oliver first kissed her, she hadn't wanted to sleep with anyone but him. The thought had never even occurred to her. And Oliver? Had he really thought her capable of cheating? He'd had no reason to. Now he was pushing her pants off, rolling onto his back. He held on to her hips, urged her up his torso toward his face. When she got there, Oliver arranged her just the way he wanted: legs spread wide just above his mouth, her knees titled precariously forward. She had to grab on to the headboard to keep her balance. Oliver was actually trying. Desperately. All because of a joke about Mr. Smiley watching her. And her saying she couldn't be stopped in any case. She couldn't figure out if Oliver was terrified she might cheat on him or excited by it. Or maybe they were the same thing after all.

Two hands on the headboard; things were getting really messy now and she wanted to bend down and grab Oliver's hair and kiss his head, but instead there was just his mouth on her and her naked body wrapped only in air and she was starting to lose it. She was also producing these unbridled sounds that made her want to bite down on something, and even though she knew Ollie loved sex and loved her and so most likely loved hearing them, she still felt a little self-conscious; it had been so long. So she held her breath and looked up at the ceiling. She saw Mr. Smiley. *If I want to take a lover, you're going to need more than Smiley here to stop me . . .* The sentence began running in a loop in her head. And the whole time, there was Oliver beneath her, finally trying. And she was actually getting close. She was the closest she'd been in forever. She felt the catch. She was about to, really, she was, but then she heard it. The *swoosh* of Oliver's phone. A text. Oliver kept going. He didn't notice at first that she wasn't there with him anymore. That she was now just a woman who was sweaty and uncomfortable and shaking, not from the anticipation of release but from having something unexpectedly snatched away. She didn't want to cry so she just kept staring up at Mr. Smiley. She swore he was laughing at her.

SO WHAT DO *you want me to do?* Maze nudged her chair lightly. Althea had been staring at her knees and, for the first time since she'd met him, completely absorbed in something else.

Sorry, I was distracted.

I'm just asking because I thought maybe your daughter had you put it up there and it might mean something.

Of course. That's what children did. But she had maintained her belief in the impossible idea that Maze didn't know she was a mother.

Um . . . no. It came with the house. I kind of think it adds character. She knew how ridiculous this sounded — of course they would have had the house repainted when they moved in — but she certainly couldn't tell Maze the truth.

So I'll just scrape it off? Like it was a piece of skin. Suddenly, she wasn't sure she wanted to get rid of Mr. Smiley. Maybe he wouldn't be visible, but he didn't have to be completely obliterated.

Actually, could you just leave it and paint over it?

There will be a bump, Maze said. *It wouldn't look good.*

Well, it's what I want.

I'm just telling you.

Okay, fine. Do whatever you think will look best.

Maze didn't say anything, just jammed his hands into his pockets and turned to walk back to the house. Althea saw that there was a rip at the hem of his shirt that hadn't been there the week before.

She read a little more but she couldn't concentrate. Why had she given in to Maze? It was such a little thing — it must have seemed that way to him, at least — and she couldn't even stand up for herself. She would just tell Maze to paint around it. If he refused, well . . . Althea now felt like she was on the verge of a panic attack. She got up, knocking *Jest* off the side of her chair, and ran to the house to catch Maze before it was too late.

She bounded up the stairs and was almost at the landing when she heard the crash.

She ran toward the master. She got to the doorway and saw Maze lying on the floor, eyes closed, gripping his right wrist.

Jesus Christ. Fuck.

The ladder had tipped over. She looked up. Mr. Smiley was still there.

Her first instinct was to turn around and pretend she hadn't seen him. She didn't want to embarrass him. She knew Maze wouldn't ever mention it. But he looked like he was really in pain.

Maze, she said. *Are you okay?* He opened his eyes, winced.

Yeah, I just cut myself on the ladder when I fell.

He wiped his wrist on his jeans.

Hold on. Althea hurried into the bathroom and began banging around, opening drawers and cabinets. She knew there had to be a first-aid kit in there somewhere. But the only remotely medical things she could find were her meds, Ollie's Advil, Bactine, and some Swedish cough drops. She ran to the closet and grabbed Ollie's Wimbledon T-shirt, the first thing she could find. She ripped it into strips and took a handful back to Maze.

He was now standing up and holding his wrist with his shirt, like it was a sling.

Would it be okay if I left early? he said.

Come here. Your wrist is a mess. Let me see. Maze hesitated, then held out his arm. She wanted to grab it close to her, kiss it. She forgot all about the argument. She took a piece of Ollie's shirt and began wrapping it around his wrist, tightly enough to stop the bleeding. He let her.

You need stitches, she said.

Nah. It's fine.

No, really. She was almost finished tying up the wound when Maze started to pull his wrist away. Althea held on just a little too long and he lost his balance and tipped into her. She put her free hand up, caught him by the shoulder. She could feel the muscles in his upper arm, tensed from holding himself up. She wanted to clutch at the fabric of his shirt, pull him closer. Or press him back, just a tiny bit, not to make him fall but to cause some sort of release. Make him unlock his body, bend his arms and knees, lie back down on the drop cloth. Signal for her to crawl on top of him. But Maze was twenty-one and cared only about getting her ceiling just right, and she was thirty-eight and married, and there was also the ladder that had fallen and the blood, all the blood. She told herself not to be ridiculous and gently righted him so he regained his balance.

Maze tilted his head to the side and narrowed his eyes, like he was trying to figure something out. They were still standing close enough together that it was almost awkward not to touch. She started pinching herself under the chin, a dubious technique she had learned in after-care. The idea was to keep you *mindful* and *grounded* in reality, in the present moment, instead of letting your emotions and thoughts about the future take you down. But now, the present moment, reality itself, was the problem. Here was Maze, not her idea of him, but Maze himself. How was she supposed to act casual about this, pretend she wasn't listening to the rhythm of his breathing or calculating the exact angle where his sneakers intersected? If Althea pinched her chin long enough, would it really stop her from doing something stupid like touching his hair, kissing his forehead? She was about to take a step back (surely that would help) when Maze reached over and peeled off a piece of painter's tape that was stuck to the cover-up she had thrown on at the pool, just above her left breast. Maze still didn't say anything; he began rolling the tape over his hip and kept looking at her. Althea blushed. She hoped that maybe if she started talking, Maze wouldn't notice.

So, um, Maze. How did you fall off the ladder? I mean, I'm sure you fell because you lost your balance. That's usually why people fall. Off ladders. And other things. That are high off the ground. So I guess the question is, why did you fall? What happened? Did something happen? Why couldn't Althea just produce a simple sentence? She always babbled in paragraphs.

I was reaching to get the sticker.

I'm so sorry, Maze. It's all my fault.

Nah. Stuff happens. You're probably gonna have to get someone else to finish the job.

What? Why?

I need both hands to paint. And I think my wrist is sprained too.

I don't want someone else, Althea wanted to say.

I can wait, she said.

It's no big deal. There's lots of other guys besides me. I'll help you find someone.

Seriously. I can wait. It's no problem.

It is for me.

Why?

Principle. Unpainted ceilings bug me.

But you're fine with letting someone else take over?

Not really. But it's better than it not getting done.

Maze, it's not going to take that long for your wrist to heal.

Never know.

Really, please.

We'll see.

ALTHEA DROVE MAZE to Southampton Hospital. She took Ollie's Porsche. She thought it would make Maze feel better. Or maybe she just hoped it would make him want to come back. They spent six hours waiting in the ER. He talked to her. He actually talked.

Things he told her: He had an older sister in college; his mom worked the checkout at IGA. His father had left when Maze was six, but he was close with his grandfather. His mother refused to cook after being around food all day so Maze made his own dinner. He loved dark chocolate with sea salt. His favorite beach was Atlantic, but he went to surf at Ditch as often as he could. He wanted to move to Oregon when he graduated and design eco-friendly houses. He also wanted to study sharks. His favorite movie was *Adaptation*. Althea wanted to ask him about the quote, but she couldn't think of how. She couldn't say, Hey, I rummaged through your wallet and found this scrap of paper and I wanted to know what it meant to you . . . So she let it be. Besides, everything she knew about Maze she had had to work for. He didn't ever just offer things up, slip the information into a narrative. Before, she'd thought he didn't talk about himself because he was shy, or maybe intimidated by their age difference. But after the Mr. Smiley incident, she knew he was more than capable of asserting himself when he wanted to.

Then she thought maybe he was just socially awkward. But really, she didn't care what the reason for his reserve was. Maze's reticence to get personal seemed like a challenge to her. He wasn't being withholding or rejecting; he just wasn't used to someone asking about him. He needed to practice. People (well, Ollie and her shrink) were always asking about her — how was her sleep, her eating, had she remembered to take the second dose of lithium — and after all these years, all their questions had made her into a person who thought and talked almost exclusively about herself. But now, here was Maze. She was thinking about him instead of herself. She was actually asking the questions, listening to the answers.

They had left it (or she had) that Maze would come by so she could pay him for the work he had done and discuss a plan for finishing the job. She was going to tell him (again) to take as long as he needed for his wrist to heal. Surely, after their time at the hospital, Maze would be willing to leave her ceiling unfinished for just a little while so he could come back and paint it himself.

Maze showed up two days later. She had to keep herself from running across the driveway to his truck as he parked. She considered whether it would now be okay to give him a hug. She was so happy, she just had to touch him. She would ask him to stay for lunch. He couldn't protest this time. At the hospital, they had eaten triangular-cut sandwiches with watery ham and American cheese they'd gotten from a vending machine. Now she knew he hated mayonnaise and liked mustard. They could even eat outside by the pool.

She walked over, but when she was halfway to him, she realized something was wrong. The truck was still idling and there was another boy sitting in the passenger seat. Her stomach dropped. She didn't want to go any farther, but she couldn't exactly turn back either, so she just stopped where she was and stood there, waiting.

Maze finally killed the engine and opened his door. His wrist was taped up; he was wearing a plain white T-shirt with a pair of tan cords and flip-flops. It was the first time she had seen him without jeans on. He didn't wave at her, just jutted his chin upward. She wanted to rush forward, grab him by the shoulders, and shake him, make him remember the time they had spent together in the hospital. Then the other door opened. She saw who it was and wanted to cry. It was Dylan from the hardware store. He was wearing a T-shirt that said CHILL, jeans so baggy they slid below the waist of his boxers, and work boots with the laces untied. Dylan put his hands on his hips and walked right up to her.

So, I hear my buddy fell down on the job. But I always stay on top of things. Promise.

He smiled and laughed at his joke. She ignored him and looked at Maze.

This is Dylan. I thought he could take over for me. He's really good.

Maze, I'm sure he is. But . . . But what? I want you?

She just couldn't work with Dylan. She could barely stand him crunching the gravel in her driveway or looking at her hydrangea bushes; she certainly couldn't have him stomping around her house, cracking jokes, splashing paint on her walls. And the problem wasn't only with Dylan. It would be the same with any other painter. Any other painter would just be someone who wasn't Maze.

. . . But I've decided to leave things as they are.

Permanently? Maze asked.

No. For now. For the summer.

Why?

She hates me, man. That's all it is. Maze kicked Dylan.

So Dylan wasn't a complete idiot. But what was she going to say? Nothing. She didn't have to say anything. It was her house. She could have stickers and unfinished ceilings and whatever she wanted. Maze didn't live there.

Seriously. Why? Maze really wanted to know, then. She had to give him a reason. Just not the real one.

I'm working on a project. I don't want any distractions.

What kind of project?

I'm a photographer. I'm preparing for a show.

Interesting, Maze said.

Maze has a thing for photographers, Dylan said.

Right, Maze said, laughing, but then he punched Dylan in the arm, so she knew he really did.

He had a girlfriend who did a whole series that she called Unnoticed Spaces; *pictures of carpets, elevator floors, shower drains, Maze . . . heavy stuff.*

How long were you together? Althea couldn't help herself.

Four hours, Dylan said.

I'm just more efficient than you are, Dyl.

Right.

So what are you thinking about? Maze asked.

Huh? she said.

About shooting? For your project? Right. Her project. What was she thinking about? Nothing. Or nothing besides Maze these days.

Um, it's about sexual desire and fantasy . . .

Wow, beats that show you dragged me to, man. Photo four: Shag Carpet with Kitty Litter Stuck in It, Dylan said.

Maze said nothing, just stared at her expectantly. She hesitated. Come on, Althea. You've been doing this forever. Just make it sound academic, she told herself.

First, I'm interested in how the sexual fantasy/desire dialectic poses the question, does desire create fantasy, or is it the other way around? In either case, the intersection of the two causes a physical tension, which increases as its release is delayed. The release is usually thought to be the orgasm. When someone orgasms, however, they are said to be coming, *i.e., still in the state of not-thereness, which would then imply that the actual release, the* arrival, *is one's state post-orgasm.* She had her head down and was staring at Maze's wrists. She couldn't believe she had said the word *coming* in front of him, but she reminded herself she was being professional, talking about her work. Maybe not her actual work, but work she could do, could have done, so it counted.

And then? Maze said. She thought he meant what comes after the post-orgasm.

It depends on your partner, I guess. She thought he would laugh. But he was actually taking her seriously.

I mean, you said first. What's the second part?

Did she have more bullshit in her? But he had never asked her so many questions. *Oh. Right. Um, the second part is . . . well, I'm still teasing it out, but basically it's about how photographs are fantasies that frequently trigger sexual desires, but they are often taken of women in order to arouse men. In my shoot, I am going to capture a man in the middle of a sexual fantasy/desire dyad so he can be the object of a fantasy/desire dyad for those looking at the picture.* Teasing it out? Dyad? High-class bullshit, but it sounded legit, she guessed.

Cool. Is he, like, going to be masturbating? Dylan asked.

No. It's not pornography.

So what, then? What's he going to be doing?

I have no idea, she thought.

Well, it's not up to me. It'll depend on the model.

Really? How will that work? Maze asked, fascinated.

Well . . . This was a hard one. But Althea was starting to believe there was actually going to be a shoot. The idea was taking shape on its own.

Um, the model's desire/fantasy is going to be evident by his expression and position, but it won't be anything so obvious as having him naked.

So he'll have to be, like, an actor? Dylan asked.

Well, sort of. He will have to be able to express his internal sensations. But they will be real, not dictated by me.

How will we know what he's fantasizing about? Unless he tells you, we won't really know, Maze said. She thought about Oliver asking to watch her masturbate before they first slept together. She thought about herself wanting to ask Maze to . . .

By use of an object. The model will bring something to the shoot that turns him on. And I will photograph him interacting, for lack of a better word, with it.

Like what? Maze asked.

Anything he wants. He just has to choose it.

Can you give an example?

Really, anything. A woman's blouse. A lipstick. What else?
She thought of his belt. *Rope.*

I want to meet the guy who gets off on lipstick. Dylan laughed
again. Maze was lost in thought.

When are you going to get started?

Never? *As soon as I find someone suitable for the work.*

Oh, Maze said. He put his hand up his shirt and began rubbing his back. Why was he always touching himself? It was
driving her crazy. She backed up two more steps. Dylan picked
up on it.

*I totally get why painting isn't your numero-uno priority right
now. But if you change your mind, I'm still in.* He shook her
hand before turning and heading back to the car.

Maze didn't move. He slid his hand around to his stomach.
She looked at his other wrist, hanging by his side.

He tipped his head down and then looked up at her. She felt
her eyes well up. Jesus, Maze.

Um . . . I hope this isn't inappropriate, but . . .

The money. She had to pay him.

No, of course not. I'll go get it. She had already counted it
out and it was sitting in a plain white envelope on her desk.

Oh, right. Well, I didn't mean that.

Oh. What, then?

Your project. I was wondering if I could do it.

Surely they were still talking about painting. She was sick
of getting it wrong. *Of course you can. I told you, I'll wait.* No;
she'd said she'd changed her mind about having the rooms
painted at all. Maybe he wouldn't call her on the difference.

No. The other one. Your shoot.

You want to model for me?

Yes.

Why?

I don't know. I like to try new things if they sound interesting.

That's all?

Pretty much.

Maze. This would be really intense. It's not just about sitting there holding something. Was she really trying to talk him out of it?

I know. That's why I want to do it.

Did you understand what I said? It's about sexual fantasy. Desire. Exposing yourself.

It might be my first time doing something like this, but I'm not stupid.

You wouldn't be embarrassed?

Probably less than you.

Well, Maze, we can give it a go. But if it turns out to be too much, we'll stop.

I won't tell you to stop.

Well, if you do —

I won't. I'm not like that . . .

I'll have to pay you.

No, you don't. It's not like I've modeled before.

Yes, I do. This is a job. It keeps the boundaries.

Okay, then. Whatever you think is fair.

I'll figure something out.

When do you want to do it?

How about Thursday night?

What do you want me to wear? I mean, it's not like I have a ton of options.

Doesn't matter. Really. Just bring the object. That's the most important thing.

Sure.

SHE SPENT THE next two days obsessing. Or, rather, obsessing more than usual. What the hell had she been thinking? She had broken her number-one rule: Never photograph anyone you know. And now she had taken on Maze. She could barely hold a conversation with him without falling all over herself; how was she possibly going to photograph him as he thought about sex? Of course, boys his age were always thinking about sex — that's what she'd read, anyway — but this time she would know he was actually doing it. He would show her what his crossing looked like — the point when his thoughts were no longer contained in his head but spread to his body — when he was visibly aroused. Would she be able to concentrate on getting the shot or would she totally lose it? Would she cry from frustration because she knew she couldn't have him in that way, or would she make an ass of herself, delude herself into thinking she could and throw herself at him? But she wasn't the only variable.

Why did Maze want to do this? She couldn't figure it out. Maybe he hadn't really understood the premise. She had made it up, sure, but by now it had become as real as any of her other shoots. She had a vision; she was going for something specific, and maybe he wouldn't be up for it. Maybe he had no idea how vulnerable he had to let himself be if it was to work and would freak out and leave when he caught on. Or maybe he understood completely and wanted another opportunity to tease her, enjoy the power he had to destabilize her just by being nearby. Maze had to be aware of how attracted she was to him, and what could be more thrilling than knowing he had done nothing but be himself to earn it. He hadn't had to pursue her or reciprocate in any way. If she left, she wouldn't be taking anything from him, because he hadn't given her anything. Even during such a shoot, he would still be in control.

Or maybe he was just curious. He wanted to be a writer. Maybe he bought into the go-to-the-edge-return-with-something-life-changing-to-write-about philosophy. As reassuring and probable as the third explanation for Maze's interest in sitting for her was, she became fixated on the show-Althea-she-can't-have-me scenario and almost called him the day of the shoot and told him not to come. But every time she went to dial, she remembered Maze standing there in her driveway, scratching his back, fiddling with his shirt. There was nothing calculated about the way he touched himself. And then there was that conversation.

Did you understand what I said? It's about sexual fantasy. Desire. Exposing yourself.

It might be my first time doing something like this, but I'm not stupid.

You wouldn't be embarrassed?

Probably less than you.

Well, Maze, we can give it a go. But if it turns out to be too much, we'll stop.

I won't tell you to stop.

Well, if you do —

I won't. I'm not like that . . .

There was no doubt. Maze knew what he was doing. He would see it through, wouldn't stop. *I'm not like that*, he had said. She didn't call him after all.

THE NIGHT OF the shoot, she sent Clem to have a sleepover with a friend from riding camp. Althea hadn't seen Clem in weeks. Well, of course she had — they lived in the same house, they ate dinner together almost every night — but she couldn't remember a thing they talked about, couldn't really even take in what Clem was wearing. Clem just annoyed her; any subject that wasn't Maze was incredibly boring and tedious.

She did talk to Ollie every night, but it was brief, like a dorm check-in, a lights-out.

She knew the only way she would keep it together when Maze arrived was to follow the routine she always did when she was working. She grabbed a large bottle of Pellegrino from the fridge, went upstairs, and changed into her work clothes: a pair of ripped cutoffs and a purple V-neck T-shirt, thin soft cotton that hit well below the waist. She never wore makeup, just a little Vaseline on her lips, and she pulled her hair back from her face in a loose ponytail. The idea was to look cool but not sexy.

She had taken some time deciding where the actual shoot should be. She had decided on a minimalist approach — just her Canon and a few gels, to limit distractions and afford some flexibility, but still, she didn't want to risk having to totally wing something once Maze got there.

She wanted the setting to function in much the same way as the object Maze was bringing; it should evoke the sexual, not so much on its own but more in how Maze interacted with it. But where should it be? The kitchen floor? The top of the pool table, his ankles in the corner pockets? The front seat of his truck, on his back, knees up, biting the steering wheel? But she wasn't supposed to stage him — wasn't that what she had said? Just let him do what he wanted. She would keep these locations in mind but ultimately see how things unfolded. Maybe she would even work around the object Maze brought. Maybe that would influence where they would go.

But the object. Jesus Christ. She hadn't let herself think about that. She was really good at not thinking about things when she didn't want to, but this . . . what was he going to bring? Really, what were the options? Probably a pair of size 0 underwear from Victoria's Secret that some girl had left in his bed. Maybe he'd even called this girl to borrow some and while they went through her drawers looking for something he thought was hot, they laughed at this middle-aged woman who wanted to take pictures of him holding it. Althea was on the part where he was sitting on the girl's bed taking off the actual bra she was wearing, white cotton with little pink hearts on it and a silk bow in the middle, and saying, *Hey, I wanna picture of that* when the doorbell rang.

He was five minutes early. Like always.

She went down to meet him, not sure whether to take her time or run.

Hello, she said, so nervous she couldn't even say his name. She gestured for him to come in. He was wearing his tan cords, a blue collared shirt, his rope belt, and a pair of white Converse. He had showered. She was touched; he had made an effort to get ready.

Hey. Here you go.

He handed her a small green plastic object the length of her index finger with a cap that slid off. It looked like a miniature home-pregnancy test. She couldn't even venture a guess.

Um, thank you. What is it?

A flash drive for the shoot. It has music on it.

Oh, of course. Thank you.

She didn't want to tell him that she didn't use music when she was working. He had probably seen it in movies: a soundtrack from Duran Duran, a girl in a bikini, the cheesy guy click-clicking. Not that Maze would know who Duran Duran was. Still, it was sweet of him to think of it.

Why don't we listen to it now? I always like to talk a bit before I start.

Um, okay. If you want . . . I just thought . . . That she would want to listen to it alone? Was he embarrassed? What kind of music had he put on there? Something with suggestive lyrics? She had to know.

Really, Maze. I usually talk to my models before the shoot to get to know them better and, more important, to get them to focus on the subject. It would be helpful to listen to the music you brought.

Oh. That makes sense.

But there's one problem.

Shoot.

I don't know how to work it.

That's easy. We can just listen to it on your laptop.

I don't have one. She handed the flash drive back. Who doesn't have a laptop? Ollie had one, Clem had one, but Althea just used the desktop upstairs in her office. Clem had probably taken hers to the sleepover, and even if she hadn't, it had horse decals all over it.

Oh. But not a big deal, right?

Of course not. I've got plenty of CDs.

Cool. He pressed the flash drive into her hand and she put it in her pocket. He had given her something. And at that moment, Althea thought there was nothing so intimate as a gift.

But where was the object Maze was supposed to bring? There was nothing else in his hands. It didn't look like there was anything in his pockets. Maybe he was embarrassed and had left it in his car? That must be it. He had just gotten there. He wasn't quite ready to show her. She wasn't going to put him on the spot. She would ask him later. After they had talked.

Let's go into the living room, Maze. Sit down. Chat. Was this really happening? Twenty-one-year-old Maze who had come to paint her walls was now following her into her house to sit on her sofa, to *chat*.

Only the glow of the pool light outside kept the living room from being completely dark. She surveyed the space. It was the perfect place to talk before they actually shot, cozy and intimate. The room had several deep couches, but she would sit on the same couch as he did, so if he got shy and started to mumble she would be able to hear what he said. She wouldn't say anything about the project at first because it might overwhelm him. Instead, she would go general with small talk before getting specific about his sex life. She walked around and turned on a lamp on each side table. She looked down at her hands and saw they were shaking. And this time it had nothing to do with her meds.

Maze just stood there, watching, hands in his back pockets.

There, Althea said, rubbing her jean shorts. Her palms were sweating. Why had she worn these jeans with the stupid rips in them? Maze didn't know this was her work outfit. He probably thought she was trying (and there was nothing worse than trying) to look hot.

Feel free to sit. Feel free? Like, what else would she expect him to do?

Maze practically fell into the couch. She was amazed at how at ease he seemed. She was almost twice his age, it was her house, and she had no idea what to say. Jesus. She knew he could sit there for hours and not say anything. It was up to her to get a conversation going.

So, Maze, do you ever get bored painting houses?

No.

What do you do in your free time?

I'm pretty much always working.

What's been your favorite project?

Hard to say.

What's it like living in East Hampton year-round?

Nothing to compare it with.

Torture. She was sure asking him about sex would be easier than trying to make small talk. But she couldn't just switch subjects so abruptly. She would offer him a drink. But what did boys like? Rum and Cokes? Tequila? She didn't have either. Well, she would just ask him and go from there.

Drink?

Sure.

What? I mean, what would you like?

Whatever you're having.

But she knew he wouldn't want Pellegrino straight from the bottle. She hadn't had a real drink in forever; Ollie always took care of that when they had guests. Then she thought of Claire. She drank red wine. Althea loved the smell of it, the way it looked as Claire twirled it in the glass, the traces that always remained on her lips and tongue. Althea imagined putting the bottle on the coffee table, pouring Maze one, two, three glasses.

How about some wine? she said.

Um, do you have any beer? Beer. Of course Maze would drink beer. College was all about beer: kegs, dark bars with sticky floors, red plastic Solo cups. Ollie drank it occasionally when they had bonfires on the beach, but Althea wasn't sure they had any.

Let me check. Don't move. Don't move? Did that sound desperate? But Maze had stretched his legs out and folded his hands behind his head. What if he fell asleep while she was gone? Would she actually get to touch him, wake him up? Surely that was allowed. But what if it really wasn't — what if he freaked out and left? She decided to give him something to do.

How about putting some music on? The stereo's over there. She had no clue how to work it and wondered if Maze did. In theory, it could blast music into all the rooms of the house and outside by the pool, but even though they had spent a fortune on it, she had never mastered it. It should keep Maze busy for the three minutes (she would hurry) it would take her to go to the kitchen and bring back a beer.

Sure, Maze said. He kicked off his shoes and stood up. The sight of him walking barefoot killed her, though; his soles touching the sisal, his ankles . . . She almost ran into the kitchen but kept herself to a brisk walk. She yanked open the door to the fridge and spotted two Heinekens in the way back, behind an apple crumb pie. She pulled them out. She took one by the neck and almost cut her finger trying to twist the cap off before realizing she needed a bottle opener. She banged around the drawers looking for the one she had used earlier on the Pellegrino. She never put things back; it could be anywhere in the house. There had to be another one somewhere. After about five minutes of frantic searching, she found one in the drawer with the knives, sitting next to a pack of Marlboro Reds. Debris from Claire's visit.

She was now so agitated, she needed something, anything, to calm her down. Maybe she would have just one cigarette. She picked up the matches that were tucked right beside the pack and was about to light up, using the fan of the Aga for ventilation, when she remembered that Oliver was the one who all but forbade her to smoke, and he wasn't there. She slid the pack into her back pocket.

Althea put some potato chips in a cut-crystal bowl she and Ollie had gotten as a wedding present and carried that and the beer to the living room. Maze was still standing by the console but there was no music.

I can't get it to work in here. But it's playing out by the pool. I've had like eight lessons on how to use it and I'm still hopeless. No big deal.

But without the music, she worried that the awkward pauses she always had around Maze would sound more, well, *awkward*. And then they would just sit there staring at each other. And then he would find her more ridiculous than he probably already did. But Maze said (he actually said):

Why don't we go outside? You know, so we can hear the music?

Althea was about to say, That's not really going to work because Frank took the cushions off the deck chairs. Or maybe, No, the mosquitoes are terrible tonight. But she stopped herself.

Great idea.

Maze slid the screen door open. Dave Matthews was playing. She loved Dave Matthews. She was trying to figure out where they should sit and where the switches for the tree lights were (she could never remember; Ollie was always the one who turned them on) when Maze walked right over to the edge of the pool, rolled up the cuffs of his pants, and stuck his feet in the water. Althea could see only the contours of his face, his body, and the bits of his hands and feet that were lit by the pool lights and the moon.

She could hear the music perfectly; it was just the right volume. For the first time with him, she didn't feel the need to talk. It was okay to just sit there.

Maze kicked his feet gently in the water. He took the beer Althea had brought him.

Do you like Heineken? Althea said, like she really expected him to say no, he didn't.

I pretty much like any kind of beer. You're not having one?

No, I take heavy doses of antipsychotics, she didn't say.

I don't drink when I'm working.

I thought I was working too, he said.

You are. But the beer's to help you relax.

I don't need alcohol to relax.

Would you mind if I smoked? she asked, pulling a cigarette from the pack.

Yes.

Althea was about to put the cigarette away but caught herself. She was sitting outside her house by her own pool and she was asking a twenty-one-year-old for permission.

Maze, it was a rhetorical question.

Well, you still asked. And I hate it.

Too bad, Althea said once the cigarette was lit and she had taken a drag.

But you're not even a real smoker.

And you would know this how?

It's obvious. You even hold it wrong.

Did you just quit or something?

No. My ex smoked. Total turnoff.

Oh. Althea wanted to put the cigarette out on her forehead. She threw the pack onto a deck chair.

Was this the photographer? Unnoticed Spaces?

Yeah.

How long were you together?

Two months.

Was it serious?

Let's just say she's pretty much been my only girlfriend.

What was it about her? That you liked?

It wasn't like I made a list or anything.

Did you love her?

I guess so.

Did you tell her?

No.

Why not?

I'm not really into that kind of thing.

But girls want to hear it.

Depends on the girl, I guess.

Don't you want to?

What?

Have someone tell you she loves you?

It's not, like, a goal of mine.

Well, what happened? Why did you break up?

I don't really look at it that way. We just stopped spending time together.

Kind of the same thing, Maze.

If you want. But it wasn't intentional. I just got really busy all of a sudden.

So you broke up with her.

I told you, it wasn't exactly like that.

Sure. Was she upset?

Dunno. I mean, she started dating someone else pretty quickly.

Do you still love her?

In a platonic way. I mean, I'm not a dick.

Althea put her cigarette out on the lip of the pool. The conversation reminded her that Maze was just a child. She had been with the same man for nineteen years and Maze hadn't even broken the two-month mark yet or said I *love you* to someone. She stood up to stretch and immediately got a head rush. She had forgotten to eat dinner. She closed her eyes and bent down to grab her knees, afraid she was going to faint. She stumbled a bit and reached for Maze's shoulder, missed, and pitched forward right into the pool.

Althea was horrified; she couldn't face Maze so she sank to the bottom of the pool. But almost immediately, there was a splash above her, and there was Maze. He grabbed her under the arms and pulled her up to the top. They broke the surface at the same time and she couldn't help studying the water running down his face. His shaving cut was gone.

Hey, he said, *are you okay?*

Perfect, she said. *I totally meant to do that. Part of my process.* Why had he come in after her? Did he really think she was such an idiot that she couldn't swim? They swam over to the side of the pool, put their elbows up on the ledge.

I came in to rescue you, Maze said. He inched a little closer to her so their hips were touching. She felt his belt digging into her side. Was this on purpose, or had the water just pushed them together? She wondered what would happen if she put her hand up under his shirt, touched his stomach.

From my own pool?

I thought you might have hurt yourself. I used to lifeguard at Main Beach. I take accidents seriously. It's dark. You might have fainted. You could have hit your head. I didn't know.

Maze ran a hand over his hair, slicked it back. Shook his head, and the excess drops hit Althea in the face. He inched away from her so they were no longer touching. So he *hadn't* meant to brush against her. She was ashamed of the assumption and looked away. Althea felt her shorts tugging her back down to the bottom of the pool; there were little patches of cold where the holes were. She felt at least twenty pounds heavier than normal and was afraid she might look it, so she decided to climb out. She pulled herself up onto the concrete, a process that was even more awkward than falling in. Why hadn't she swum to the ladder? Her body left a shadow of wet on the ground, and when she stood up, her T-shirt was almost see-through. She was wearing a bra, but when she looked down, she saw her nipples pressing against the fabric. She folded her arms across her chest. Maze pushed off the wall and did a back-flip under the water. She waited for him to come up.

I'm going to grab some towels from the pool house. Be right back. Then we should get to work.

Sure.

Althea walked away from him. Then she heard the *thwack* and looked back.

Maze had taken off his shirt, thrown it out of the pool. Jesus. His lower body was hidden below the water, so it looked like he was naked. He had muscles, but the kind that made his frame look chiseled, not bulky. She tried to keep walking — she was supposed to be getting towels, after all — but it was impossible; Maze was mesmerizing. So she waited. Maze sat on the stairs of the pool and let his legs float up to the surface. He bent his head down, undid his belt, pulled off his cords, and tossed them into a pile next to the shirt. He ducked under the water and started to breaststroke. Not rushing or racing, just enjoying being surrounded, enveloped by the water.

He had left his boxers on — she could see them in the pool lights, plain blue — and she was relieved. She had photographed plenty of nude bodies before, but this was different. She didn't want him to be just another naked body. A gorgeous naked body, yes, but no, she didn't want that. Maze in his boxers meant there was still innocence (I'm just doing laps in the pool), curiosity (what would it be like to, well, *you know*), and desire (hers or his? That was the mystery).

She finally forced herself to turn away. She went to the back of the pool house and took two white towels from the stack on the counter. She was freezing and decided to leave Maze in the pool just a little longer so she could take a shower. There was shampoo, conditioner, vanilla-almond body butter, and a comb and two robes in the pool house by the outdoor shower. She unzipped her wet cutoffs and was about to peel them off when she felt a tiny bulge in the pocket. She reached in and pulled it out: Maze's flash drive. She clutched it in her hand as she removed the rest of her clothes. Standing naked, she held it up to her face. It was beautiful, really, the clear green plastic, compact and hard as a bullet. She drew it across her cheek; it was slippery and cool from being in the pool. She brought it to her mouth and kissed it. She knew the thing was probably damaged past the point of repair, that she would probably never hear Maze's mix, but it didn't matter. Maze had given it to her. He had gone to some store and taken money from his wallet (Jesus, that wallet), paid for it, stuck it into his computer with his hands, and put music on it for her.

She took it from her mouth and ran it down her neck, over her collarbones. Then she slid it under and around her breasts, up and down her ribs, across her lower stomach, then to her groin, right to left, right to left, then lower. She started pressing so hard it surprised her, and then, and then (well, she was totally distracted) she leaned back against the wooden planks of the pool-house wall and circled her fingers (the ones not holding the drive) around her sweet spot, the place she hadn't touched in forever, and pushed them in and out of herself. She clutched it the whole time, the green plastic thing Maze had given her, and soon she was so wrecked (she had gone there and come back), she wasn't sure she could collect herself and return to the pool. He would see her, and he would know. Of course he would. That drive was more than a drive; it was also Maze himself — at least, in the pool house it was. She decided to prolong the experience and take a shower.

She went back outside wearing a robe, tightly belted, with the drive tucked in her pocket.

Maze was sitting on the edge of the pool, kicking up water and leaning on his elbows.

All good?

Yes. Why?

You've been gone for like twenty minutes. I was about to come check on you.

Oh. Right. I guess I was. Sorry. I take long showers.

For once, Althea was glad he didn't ask a lot of questions.

Is it okay if I go and take one?

Of course. For the first time that night, she felt almost relaxed, but then she saw the pile of wet clothes on the ground at her feet and realized that once again there was something to be worried about. Maze needed to be dressed for the shoot. She couldn't ask him to put his wet clothes back on, and he certainly couldn't borrow any of Oliver's. She would just have to put Maze's things in the dryer. If she could figure out how to work it.

Great. See you in a sec. Maze stood up, began rubbing the water out of one ear. That's when she noticed it. There was a tiny red scar on his right biceps. It was nothing, really, but she was overcome with desire. She wondered if they could possibly stand there just a little bit longer, facing each other, Maze in his wet boxers, her touching the scar. In case nothing else happened that night, in case she couldn't work the dryer or something else went wrong and she had to send him home, she would at least have the memory of his scar rising under her fingers. It would be better than a kiss; Maze had probably kissed lots of girls, or maybe just a few, but still, Althea knew none of them had spent any real time exploring that scar.

But Maze walked away from her and she went down to the basement to face the dryer. She was surprised by how manageable it turned out to be. She opened the top, dumped the clothes in, put it on high for sixty minutes. Sixty minutes seemed like forever, but it would give them time to talk.

She rushed up the stairs to her room to change out of the robe she had on. She wanted to be ready when Maze finished his shower. Another dilemma. What was she going to wear? As she flipped through the rack, she realized that the thing that fit best and seemed the most appropriate for the occasion was a long black linen dress. The only problem was that it had a T-back and she couldn't wear a bra. She normally wore it only when she was alone, but it was so comfortable, she would just trust that it wouldn't look too provocative to Maze if, again, her nipples poked out.

She slipped the dress over her head. She usually wore whatever pair of underwear she pulled first from the drawer, but this time when she put them on (why had this never bothered her before?), she noticed she could clearly see the lines of the underwear underneath the dress. The only thing left to the imagination was their color. She didn't own any thongs (except for the hateful one she had bought at Bonne Nuit, and she certainly wouldn't wear that ever again) and she wasn't going to spend the rest of the night stuffed into sheer pantyhose. So she decided to wear nothing.

When she got back to the living room, Maze was sitting on the couch with a towel wrapped around his waist. The room was dim. She could see his boxers hanging over the back of a chair. Dave Matthews was still playing.

Hey. I killed the outside lights and flipped these on. Hope that's okay.

Of course, but how did you get the music to work in here?

Ah, wasn't that hard after all. I can show you.

No, no, it's okay. Stay where you are. She didn't want his towel to slip off. What could she possibly do if his towel slipped off? *Didn't you see the robes hanging on the back of the door?* she said as she sat down next to him.

I'm not really into robes.

Oh.

Maze was silent. Then:

Is your husband cool with all of this?

All of what?

Tonight . . . I mean . . . Here he was, sitting next to her wrapped in a towel, torso bared, skin still hot from the water (well, this was what she imagined), Dave Matthews playing, and he was worried if Oliver was *cool with all of this?* She almost fell off the couch. Was Maze thinking the same thing she was?

I'm not sure I follow, Maze.

The shoot. I mean, it's kinda, you know . . . Of course. The shoot. That's what he was referring to. Nothing to do with them. At least, nothing personal. Why on earth would Maze think of her that way? He was a *fucking boy.* She felt totally humiliated.

Let me ask you this. What does your mom think?

Huh?

You seem to be extremely concerned about getting permission.

No . . . I'm just trying to understand. I mean . . . what your situation is.

I don't have one.

Everyone does.

Maze, we're working together.

I didn't mean to upset you. I just wanted to know.

Maze, I'm a grownup. Which basically means I get to do what I want.

Oh. Glad I checked. He shifted a tiny bit on the couch and reached for his beer.

AN HOUR LATER, she went to the basement to check on Maze's clothes. They were hot. She wondered how long they had been dry. It was now midnight. He had finished both beers and then switched to wine. They had been talking about Maze's sex life. Even though his answers were brief, they increased her desire and her frustration simultaneously, and the tension was driving her insane.

Have you slept with a lot of girls?

Define a lot.

Put it this way: How many girls have you slept with?

Seven.

When did you lose your virginity?
Fifteen.
Was it a good experience?
Yeah. It could have been better for her, maybe.
Do you masturbate?
Like everyone else.
I mean, do you do it often?
Sure.
What do you think about when you masturbate?
Women.
Any specific women?
Sure.
Any specific women that come to mind now?
Sure.
Do you want to tell me who?
Nope.
Does it take you a long time to come?
What?
Does it take you a long time to come?
If I'm in the mood, which I usually am if I'm doing it, no.
What happens when you do it?
What do you mean?
Do you close your eyes or say anything?
Yes to closing my eyes. No to saying anything.
Even during sex?
Definitely not during sex.
Would you go down on a girl?
It's not like I mind it.
But . . .
Nothing. It's not like I mind it. At all.

She had to get behind the lens, put some distance between the two of them. She still had to ask for the object — God, she was terrified the object would finish her off. She now imagined it would be like asking Maze to bring another girl to her house and then watching them fuck. What had she been thinking? He would be touching it, holding it, and thinking about a woman — he said he always thought about a woman — who was not her. But it wasn't like she could send him home now.

She came up from the basement with his clothes folded in her arms. She handed them over.

You can use the powder room. She pointed, even though the door was visible from the couch. Maze stood up, took a step, and banged his shin on the coffee table.

Whoops. He stumbled a bit, then righted himself. She wondered if it would bruise. He shifted his cords and his shirt in his arms but still looked right at her before turning and walking away to get dressed.

Better? she asked when he came back.

Actually, I'd rather spend my life in a towel. Much more comfortable. He laughed. Althea was so distracted by the thought of seeing this boy in a towel every day, she couldn't think of anything to say.

So . . . what's next? he said.

We shoot. But first, the object. You have to give me your object.

I already did.

Huh? When?

The flash drive. That was it.

And Althea had thought it was a gift for her. That he had made a mix, chosen music for her. How the idea had turned her on — enough to get herself off in the shower. Now she felt like an idiot. He'd brought it only because she'd told him to. She couldn't let him use it for the shoot. It made her too sad.

Oh, right. I didn't realize it, I'm sorry. It's too small to work.

Well, you said lipstick was okay.

True, but even if I manage to get it on film, no one will know what it is.

Does it matter? It thought it was supposed to be specific just to me.

Yes, it does matter. Actually, it didn't, Althea knew. But she had to talk him out of it.

Why?

Umm, well, let's think about this. What about the drive turns you on? The color? The feel? Could she really go through this again? Hearing what made him hard?

It's not the drive. It's what's on it. The music.

So it references something that references something.

I guess so.

That's very meta, Maze, but we can't represent it visually. People won't get it.

Do they have to know it's music? Can't they just see my reaction to it? Wasn't that the point?

Part of it. But the object was supposed to be something more sexual, I guess.

Cliché, you mean. Underwear. Or handcuffs.

Not necessarily . . .

Yes, that's what you're saying . . .

Maze, let's just use something else.

No. This is what I want to use. Anything else would be contrived.

I'm sure we could find something.

Look, I'm not really into objects in the first place. It took me a long time to come up with this.

I'm not saying you have to develop some kind of fetish, and I'm not criticizing what you brought. I just think we can find something that will work better. Once we get started, you won't care about the object. It will just be you and your thoughts.

Fine. Let's do underwear, then. I think I can work with that.

Good idea. Then she realized the only underwear in the house was hers.

Actually, maybe you're right. Maybe underwear is cliché. There's got to be something else. A blanket, maybe? A pillow?

Nah, said Maze.

A peach?

Messy. And kinda random.

A DVD with a provocative film on it?

Definitely not.

I'm running out of ideas here, Maze. Can you help me out?

Sure. I've got something that will work.

What's that?

Your dress.

My dress? Why?

I'm into linen.

Oh. That was all she could say. *Oh.*

Let me run upstairs and change.

Don't.

Huh?

Don't go anywhere.

I need something to change into, Maze.

No, you're missing the point.

And that would be?

Maze didn't say anything.

She backed away, speechless. Was he serious? Maze sat down on the couch, waiting. Then he said:

Do you have to get permission or something? He was teasing her, but he definitely wasn't kidding.

Of course not . . .

Althea walked over to the couch.

Maze gently put his arm around her lower back and pulled her into his face. She could almost feel him breathing through the material of her dress. He kissed her left hipbone, moved his mouth across her lower stomach, then kissed the right. She wanted to press herself into him, she really did, she was holding on to his shoulders now, those shoulders, and it would have been so easy. But she saw that collar, the blue collar of his oxford, and she wanted to touch his neck, slide her hands down into his shirt, feel his back. She decided to wait, just a second, or a minute, or whatever it took, and let Maze — *Jesus*, he had now pushed her dress up and was sliding his hands up and down her chest, tracing his fingers over her stomach — take the lead, do what he wanted.

He was methodical, Maze, as a painter. She knew he would have a plan for doing things; he would not be all over the place. After he finished with her stomach, he took his hands out from under her dress, walked his fingers up her arms, stood up, and started kissing — no, it was sucking, really — the side of her neck. His head was tucked under her jaw. She took his chin in both of her hands, cradled it. And there it was again.

Right there. His collar. She couldn't take it. She needed to get the shirt off. She needed to touch his back. His chest. Most of all, his scar.

But then Maze put his arms below Althea's shoulder blades and pulled her into him, and she could feel his hardness. She so wanted to envelop him with her mouth. Taste the salt and sweat. Glide the skin smoothly up and down with her hand, quickly, slowly, quickly. She wanted to suck on the tip, rub him gently across her lips, around her face, feel him swell at the touch.

She would lick and kiss the base of his penis, make it throb. Then the ecstasy — what else to call it? She simply wanted to make him come. And then she wanted to watch him as he lay there, spent, and looked at her or at the ceiling and had Maze thoughts, which he would probably keep to himself, but he would be warm and sleepy and happy and that would be enough.

But what about after? What would she think about as she watched him, naked and vulnerable, lying on the couch; what would she think about during that sweet pause (the bliss), after the oblivion and before the coming-to, when anything was still possible? Would she want him to stay? Spend the entire night and sleep in her house, stay with her forever? Would she want to hide his clothes and take away his cell phone and lock the windows so he would have to stay? But maybe she wouldn't think that. Maybe she would remind herself that Maze was a boy and even though he had wanted her to touch him, and she had wanted to, he had to leave, go back home, go back to the forward that was still coming for him. She would know his leaving had nothing to do with her, even if he never came back.

She would try to make herself feel better by telling herself she was the one who had gotten the most out of the situation. He had allowed her to be a woman like any other. He didn't know about any of it, the Visions or the Tombs. And she doubted that Maze would care even if he did. But was it okay to love someone partly for this? Not for how they were, but for how they thought of you? She couldn't bear the thought of using Maze. But then she was back to the question: What if they went through with things tonight and she couldn't handle his leaving? Even if he said it meant something. What if she came apart?

Or what if, afterward, she thought about Oliver? What if just as she was feeling an ache in her jaw from all that work on Maze, on *his* . . . what if she remembered then that she had a husband, a husband who had packed the purple duffle for all of her visits to NY-Pres. Who knew not to bring headphones. *Who cheated on her.* Who knew all the times she had been there so he could tell the attending and make sure the charts were filled out properly so she didn't have to. *Who cheated on her.* Who wrapped up her wrists. *Who cheated on her.* And now here she was, cheating on him. Or cheating him. And she would wonder what the difference was between the two. He was guilty of the former and she the latter, but now she had done both.

And what about Clem? Wouldn't Althea think about Clem? This was the first summer she had been determined not to cheat Clem. Had planned to spend time with her, get to know her better. And she had done none of that. Once again, Clem was off the stage of Althea's life, off at riding camp during the day and being looked after by the housekeeper's daughter at night, and they'd barely been out there a month. Althea had been too preoccupied with a boy only eleven years older than Clem. Even if Clem didn't find out about Maze, even if she never knew, Althea would be cheating her. Because for the rest of the summer, Althea would be seeing Maze, thinking about seeing Maze, or remembering what it was like to see Maze.

Or what if things bumbled on with Oliver and Clem but Maze woke up and hated her? What if he noticed the frame Clem had made out of driftwood and shells sitting on the coffee table, or the needlepoint pillow that her mother had made with *Mr. and Mrs. Oliver Holden Willow* and their wedding date stitched on it lying on the chair? And he would think what a horrible person she was. Not only did she have no regard for her family, but she had taken advantage of him. Seduced him. She had said, Have a drink, Maze. Take a shower, Maze. Tell me what you think about when you masturbate, Maze; what makes you want to come? What was he supposed to do?

But what about the happy ending? Lying next to Maze with her head on his chest and her hand on his stomach, touching (very lightly, so she wouldn't wake him) the thin line of hair that ran from his bellybutton to down below his hips? How intoxicated she was by the smell of Maze's skin, the sound of his breathing, the sight of his — his anything . . . What about her thinking about what they were going to do when he woke up? Of course they would eat . . . but what? Wearing what? It would be three in the morning . . . And what was she going to say to him? Would she tease him or whisper something sweet?

And what would he say after such an incredible, intimate, and intense experience?

And as Maze kept *touching* her and she felt it through her dress, Althea had a harder and harder time staying with the two-of-them-on-the-couch-swapping-intimacies scenario. No, standing there, with Maze's arms around her back, pushing himself into her, she just thought about the other possibilities, the other endings. The miserable ones. Miserable for Oliver, Clem, and Maze. Miserable for her.

Althea reached behind her back for his hands (was she really doing this?), pulled them in front of her. Held them together so he couldn't touch her anymore. But then Maze leaned in and kissed her. Kissed her mouth. It was the first time he had. It was different than his kissing her neck or her stomach. He didn't gently slide his tongue into her mouth, acknowledge the boundaries between the two of them; instead, he pushed it in, tangling it up in hers, pausing only to suck on her lips until they were as swollen as blisters and her cheeks were chafed red from rubbing against his unshaven skin.

She thought of this type of kissing as a *famishing*; the more she kissed Maze, the hungrier he made her.

But then Maze removed his mouth from hers and pulled his oxford out of the waist of his cords. Undid his belt. The rope one. She put her hands up Maze's back. She remembered how it had looked in the pool, in the towel, earlier that night. She had had hours to study it. The V it made to the waist, the sharp shoulder blades, the muscles running just below. But touching it was ecstasy. It was like diving into a wave, putting her head under, and feeling the salt on her face, rather than just walking along the shore break. He finished unbuttoning his oxford and took off his shirt. And there it was. On the top of his right biceps. The scar.

Althea stopped rubbing his back. She stopped everything. She didn't know what to do. It was such a private thing, a memory etched on his arm. What had happened? She had to know. She couldn't go any further until she asked him.

Maze? He was busy unbuttoning his cords. She remembered his boxers were still out drying by the pool. She was glad she had gotten to the scar before he removed the pants. She wouldn't have been able to say anything had he removed his pants.

Mmm? He didn't look up.

Maze, she said a little more loudly. He stopped working on the buttons.

Huh?

She was suddenly shy. What if he wouldn't tell her?

What happened to your arm? I mean, why do you have that scar? She nodded toward it, still not letting herself touch it. He put his hand over it.

Oh. That. I walked through a pane of glass. Never got it stitched up.

Did it hurt?

Nah.

Oh. Good. Can I touch it?

He laughed. Here he was, on the verge of taking his pants off. *Sure.*

She reached over, patted it with her fingers. It felt like skin. Just Maze's skin, after all that. But despite his explanation, given with his usual indifference, a cut still hurt. She had seen him that day he had fallen off the ladder. She couldn't bear to think of him in pain. He didn't know, couldn't know, what he was getting into, could he? He was just a boy.

She removed her fingers from Maze's scar and took a step back so their toes were no longer touching. She smoothed down her dress and straightened the straps. She reached over and buttoned up his pants, picked his shirt up from the couch. He looked at her, asking the question. She didn't say anything, didn't even shake her head. She was afraid if she did, she would give in again, and then she wouldn't be able to stop herself. But Maze, being Maze, understood.

He went to take his shirt from her, but she wanted to put it on him, wanted to do up the buttons that he had just undone. She didn't know if she would ever get to touch Maze again. She didn't know if she would ever see him again. He didn't seem like the type to give second chances. She took her time on each button, pushing it slowly through the small hole, making sure all parts of it were through. She rubbed the rough cotton of the oxford as her fingers climbed up the shirt. She was dreading getting to the top, to just below the collar, the place that had once seemed so thrilling.

He stood there and let her dress him. Maze, she knew, wasn't afraid of silence, didn't need to talk this over. When she was finished with his shirt, he picked up his belt from the floor and went to tuck it in his back pocket. She knew she couldn't put it on him, couldn't even touch it. She wanted to. Jesus, she wanted to. And after everything she had done, it would be cruel to ask him for a souvenir. She had to send him away intact.

Once he was finished, she wasn't sure what to do next. At first, it seemed she had two options: fall on the ground and beg forgiveness, or speed the goodbye so she could go in the kitchen and cut herself. But she managed to find a third.

Maze, this is awkward, but . . .

No worries. He scratched his forehead.

It's hard to explain, but I . . .

No need.

I just want you to know it's not your fault.

I didn't think it was.

He reached over and adjusted the strap on her dress. His fingers were on her shoulder for only a few seconds, but it felt like an eternity.

Maze?

Yeah?

I'm also sorry I ruined the shoot. I know you really wanted to do it.

Not really.

Huh?

Well, actually, I thought the subject was pretty depressing.

You think sex is depressing?

No. Wanting it instead of having it is.

Oh. I can see your point.

I've gotta go.

Okay. She wanted to ask, Go where? just to have him stand there a little bit longer, but she knew she didn't really have the right. *I'll walk you out.*

I got it. Should she insist, follow him? He started to walk away without so much as a hug.

Maze . . .

Yeah? He turned back.

Am I ever going to see you again? I mean, just because we lost control —

I never lose control.

Oh. Of course not. And he left, without answering her question.

SHE WENT BACK and sat down on the couch, the couch of their Almost. Thinking about it was ecstasy and hell. Her stomach ached and she wanted to cry, but somehow, at the same time, the memory of it aroused her so much she was tempted to put her hand underneath her dress. She finally fell asleep around four, after the unrelenting tension had completely exhausted her. She woke two hours later to someone shaking her shoulder. Clem.

Lune. Are you okay?

No, I'm not. I sent away the most beautiful boy just as we were about to have sex.

Aren't you supposed to be at the Crearys'? Althea said instead. *I thought they were going to drop you at camp.*

I forgot my crop. I called you like five times this morning and you didn't pick up.

Oh. I must have turned my phone off last night. I was working.

Of course she had turned it off.

I thought something was wrong.

Like what?

Clem ignored the question. *I called Daddy. He tried to reach you too. Then he said he was coming out.*

What? Why? Just because I didn't answer my phone?

You need to call him.

Jesus. Let me get my phone.

Lune?

Yes?

After you talk to him, can you help me find my crop?

Sure.

And drive me to camp?

We'll see.

She ran up to her room. She had to reach Oliver before he left. She couldn't see him, not this morning with her head full of Maze. She had already planned to have Clem spend another night at the Crearys'. She would have sent her there for the whole week if she could have.

Hey, Ollie. It's me.

Jesus, Althea. Are you all right?

Fine.

I've been calling you for the past hour. What the hell is going on?

Nothing. I turned my phone off last night and forgot to turn it back on. I was in the middle of a new project. I was fucking around with a boy half my age.

You can't just turn your phone off. I need to be able to reach you.

Well, I had to concentrate. It's fairly complicated.

Althea, you have to tell me if you were thinking about hurting yourself.

I wasn't.

You haven't worked in about two years.

Well, I was last night.

You haven't told me about any work until now.

Well, that's because you're still mad at me. About Claire.

Let's not talk about her right now.

Why?

Because it still upsets me.

That she threw an ice cream maker at my head?

Althea, you know it's the principle of it.

What principle?

You don't just fire people on a whim.

It wasn't on a whim.

You didn't have a valid reason. You didn't give her a warning. She was wearing her nightgown when you did it.

She was at the house for two weeks and got nothing done. I think that's a reason.

Althea, you take so many meds, your judgment is always clouded. You need to let me make these decisions.

Really.

Really.

Fuck you, Oliver.

Althea. I don't know what you were doing last night, but you don't sound like yourself. I'm coming out.

Please don't.

Wow. You're unbelievable. Just keep your phone on.

After she hung up, she wanted to go into the guest room and get in bed. She wasn't really tired, she just wanted to be alone with her Maze thoughts, immersed in the fantasy. She heard

Clem yelling for her to help find her crop, but she just put the pillow over her head and ignored her.

ON MONDAY, four days since she had buttoned up Maze's shirt, four days since she had watched him put his rope belt in the back pocket of his pants, Althea was still beside herself. She couldn't stop thinking about him. *Would you go down on a girl? . . . It's not like I mind it. At all.* She had to explain . . . what? That she'd been an idiot? That she had to see him? Oliver was right. She did have crappy judgment. She picked up her phone and dialed. It went to voicemail.

It's Maze. Leave a message. I'll call you back. She wondered if he would.

I need to talk to you. That was all she said. What else was there?

And then came the waiting. Althea checked her phone every three minutes. Nothing. She told herself Maze was going to call. Of course he was. But she couldn't just sit on the couch all day. She needed a project. She decided to go into town and buy something for Maze.

She didn't have any credit cards of her own. Ollie had taken them away after a Visions episode five years ago when she had spent twenty-five thousand dollars in two weeks. He admitted this actually was impressive because almost everything she brought home was complete crap. E-bay, Etsy madness, and also Indian jewelry, coin collections, hoodies with the names of her favorite cities, whole sets of celebrity cookbooks, et cetera, et cetera, et cetera. She had paid for it all out of her own accounts, but still. Now, he had to authorize any purchase over a certain amount, and he always went over the bills (or said he did) to see if there was any unusual activity. So would he notice if she bought a man's bathing suit? Couldn't she just tell him it was a present for him that she had lost? But he liked only Cuillet bathing suits from Saint-Tropez. Why would she buy Maze one at Khanh Sports? She could take out money from the ATM and pay cash. She still got money deposited into her bank account every month from her trust in California. But buying Maze something with a wad of cash seemed wrong somehow, like she was renting a hotel room by the hour. So, no to the swimsuit. But Althea was determined to give him something, something she wouldn't have to charge on her husband's card, that Maze would like. Then she remembered the flash drive. She would make him a mix.

She went to her office and spent three hours on her desktop choosing the songs. It was the first mix she had made since college, before drag-and-drop, before burning, before even CDs. She listened to every song at least four times before deciding. They were all about craving. Merging. Bliss. There were no dark ones. Nothing to come back from. In the end, she had a list of thirty-six songs.

Althea didn't have a flash drive so she decided to go to Staples in Bridge to buy one. She had had her phone next to her the whole time, sitting there on her desk, ringer on high so she could hear it over the music, but nothing. She started to wonder if Dylan had told him not to call. *Dude, she's ancient.*

And a head case. Or, worse, if Maze had gone out and picked up some random girl at Talkhouse. But really, Althea told herself, there was no other girl. Not yet, anyway. She just had to wait.

She got in her car, put her cell in the cup holder, and began the drive west to Bridgehampton Commons. Cars were crawling down 27. She should have put on her headphones and walked. She got to Staples almost forty-five minutes later. The parking lot was packed. People shopping at King Kullen for groceries, Kmart for patio furniture, or Williams-Sonoma for special pumpkin butter and waffle makers. Grown-up things for their houses. For their families and kids. And here Althea was, picking up a flash drive for a mix she had compiled for a twenty-one-year-old boy.

Inside Staples, the air was as solid and cold as a block of ice. Althea wandered around the aisles looking for the flash drives. Ridiculously, she took a cart. Well, it wasn't like she couldn't buy some other things, she told herself, and kill some more time. She picked up drawing supplies for Clem and printer paper and pens for Oliver.

Her shopping cart had a loose wheel and made a loud, annoying noise as she navigated the aisles. Pushing it was much harder than it should have been, but Althea was so consumed by her own thoughts that she didn't even notice. Then she heard, *Althea! Hey!* Her heart lurched, but of course it wasn't him. Maze never used her name or spoke in exclamation points. So there she was, flushed and looking like an idiot, pushing a broken shopping cart, buying a flash drive for Maze. She took her time turning around to Dylan. Dylan and some girl. Not the girl from the hardware store, but of that same tribe. She and Dylan were standing by the refrigerator case rifling through the bottles of Coke, checking out the names on the labels, part of Coke's new marketing campaign: *Share a Coke with Melissa. With Andreas. With Doug.*

Why don't they ever have Jenna? The girl with Dylan was pretty. Not exactly gorgeous, but fresh.

They never have Jenna, she said. Althea wanted to keep shopping, but she left the cart where it was and walked over. To avoid them would be immature. At thirty-eight, she should be past that. But, more important, Dylan was a friend of Maze's. She had to find out if Maze had told him anything.

Dylan. What a coincidence. She didn't look at Jenna, who was still searching the Coke bottles for her name. But Dylan didn't bother introducing her. Althea guessed the relationship was just beginning or just ending. *How are you?*

Day off. Lots of work. I'm painting a six-bedroom in Bridge. You?

Just buying a flash drive so I can make Maze a mix. *Proofs of the shoot.*

Right. How'd it go?

It was probably the best head-fuck he ever had, she thought. Instead: *The whole thing went really well. Maze seemed pretty comfortable. It didn't take long to finish.*

Never does for him. She had such a horrified look on her face that Dylan actually said, *Sorry, it's a running joke. Bad taste.* She wanted to cry. But he made her remember that Maze was only twenty-one. Still thought jokes like that were funny. Of course Maze wasn't going to call her back. At his age, you didn't call hookups back. You just didn't. All of a sudden, she had a strong desire to ask Jenna if they could talk privately and then ask her advice. Should she text Maze? Call him again? But that was about as low as Althea could go. She might as well call Oliver and ask him what *he* thought of the whole situation.

Jenna turned back to them clutching a bottle that said *Share a Coke with Jennifer.*

Finally! Everyone calls me Jenna, but it's just a nickname for Jenniffer, two f's, but still. Jennifer counts. I'm so psyched.

I bet they don't even make my name, Althea said, joking. But she didn't say it quite right, and it came out sad. Jenna looked sympathetic, acknowledged that was probably true.

It's still a cool name, she said.

I like it. She wanted to snatch the Jennifer bottle and throw it at Dylan's head to get him to continue their conversation; he was currently distracted by a bin of patterned duct tape. Instead, she walked over and scooped up a few handfuls and put them in the cart.

Whoa — why are you getting so many?

When I'm not shooting, I make stuff with it.

Like what?

Hard to describe. It always is, Althea.

Oh, got it. Dylan smiled. Not those kind of things, she wanted to say.

Well, like dollhouses, but not sweet ones. I cover the walls and floors in duct tape. I wanted to do my house that way, but apparently it would take too many rolls, and no one would be willing to do it —

Maze would.

You wouldn't?

Nah. I'm not that patient. Maze would actually get off on it. Lining up the strips, over and over, hours and hours by himself, making it all perfect. You know I love the guy, but he's a head case.

Why do you say that?

He just is. And I was really surprised he did the shoot. He hates to be told what to do. Total control freak. Must be something about you. Or maybe he hit his head when he fell off that ladder of yours.

Right. Well, I've got a lot to do, Althea said, trying an easy laugh and moving away, though of course she could have stood there all day talking to Dylan about Maze.

Yeah, sure. Take care.

WHEN SHE FINALLY headed back to the house, she had a huge number of bags in the trunk. After buying art supplies for Clem and office supplies for Oliver at the Staples (she ended up filling her cart), she had gone to Kmart and bought tiki lamps, a hammock, woolen blankets. Then she went to King Kullen for Pellegrino, beer, and coconut sorbet. She also bought sliced turkey, ham, Swiss cheese, and seven-grain bread. She stopped at a farm stand and bought raspberries, peaches, tomatoes, mozzarella, basil, corn salad, milk, eggs, guacamole, and blueberry pie.

After the farm stand, she kept driving until she was in town.

There were some things she just had to have. They were expensive, and Oliver might say she didn't need them, but he wouldn't be able to say it was like the Visions shopping. That had to do with frenzied theories and random accumulation. This was different; she had clarity, she knew what she was doing. She needed to buy new sheets, not the ones she and Ollie had slept on. She wanted to get linen ones and new down pillows. And maybe a cashmere throw.

And new lingerie. Not the slutty kind she had gotten to seduce Oliver. The kind that came in pretty colors, like peony pink and moss green, or just plain white; the kind with delicate lace and hand-sewn flowers that would leave the stretch of her stomach bare and ready for Maze's hands to touch or his mouth to kiss on his way up to her chest or down, down to wherever he wanted to go. She suddenly didn't have a problem using Ollie's cards to pay.

She bought it all. The lingerie and the sheets. The sheets came in huge shopping bags. She bought two sets — no one bought one set of sheets, after all — four king pillows, and a cream throw. She also bought a duvet cover, a new duvet, and a few throw pillows. The lingerie came in one tiny bag with tissue paper. It cost almost as much as the sheets.

Walking back to the car, she passed by the hardware store. She wondered if Hal was working and if he would know where Maze was. Maybe Maze was at the beach. Surely that was why he hadn't called. She saw the ladders in the window. Thought of Maze. If he hadn't fallen that day, trying to scrape Mr. Smiley off the ceiling, she wouldn't be holding bags of sheets and lingerie. She wondered if he realized that. Maybe she could find him a miniature ladder and give it to him when she saw him again?

Didn't all couples do that? Reference their beginnings with little gifts? Turn them into a story? Maybe she would have to explain it to him. But that was okay. It was Maze. She could do that. He wouldn't think it was stupid. But where would she get such a thing? The Internet, on eBay? Possibly, but that would take too long.

What about Mr. Smiley? She could get him a packet of stickers. They must still sell them at the Party Store. But Mr. Smiley represented Oliver watching over her. Making sure she was safe. Keeping her faithful (as the joke went). Although nothing had to do with Oliver anymore. He didn't want to sleep with her. He was spending the summer in the city to punish her. Why shouldn't she appropriate Mr. Smiley? Maze took her projects seriously: Repainting the house. Her shoot. Their almost-sex. There was nothing cynical or judgmental about him. Even when she failed. And she had failed at all three, hadn't she?

And so she went to the Party Store to buy three packets of Mr. Smiley stickers. She would stick them on the color strip she had gotten for the bedroom and tell him he could use it as a bookmark.

Just as she reached the entrance, just as she was pushing the door open, her phone rang. She scurried out into the parking lot, dug the phone out of her purse, and slammed it to her cheek. She took a breath and told herself she would just say his name, not turn it into a question. Not *Maze?* but *Maze.* Then he would say, *Yeah?* and she would ask him to come over that night. She would figure out what to do with Clem later.

She felt surprisingly calm and managed to say softly, almost in a whisper, *Maze.*

But instead of the mellow and casual *Hey* or *What's up* that Althea was expecting, the voice she heard was loud and angry. She was so caught off-guard it took her a second to translate the sounds into words.

Althea? Where are you?

Oliver. Oliver was what she had in her life. Althea was so stunned, she couldn't say anything.

Althea? Who — or what — is Maze?

Maze, he's, um, the boy who came to paint the house.

Well, he didn't do a very good job.

It's not done.

That's a relief. Do you have a time frame?

What are you talking about?

The ceiling of the bedroom is the same color as before. Didn't you think I'd notice?

Where are you?

At the house.

At our house?

Yes, our house.

I told you I'm fine.

I didn't come just to see you. But that would be nice.

I know. I mean, I want to see you too, of course. I'm just doing a few errands.

I don't mean to inconvenience you.

Stop it.

I've been on the jitney for three hours. I just wanted to come home and relax, and my wife is MIA and my ceiling is fucked up.

Ollie, I'll be home when I'm done.

Don't kill yourself.

WHEN SHE GOT back to the house, Oliver was sitting on the front steps reading the *WSJ* wearing jeans, Claire's *Crépuscule* belt, a salmon-pink polo, and a pair of yellow-and-orange Spectacle shades that Althea didn't recognize. His hair was longer than when he'd left and he needed a haircut. It looked like it had in college, and maybe that was the point. It was at least eighty-five degrees outside. She wondered why he wasn't in the house getting settled. But when he looked up, Althea realized by the way he clenched his jaw that he really was furious at her. She left her shopping bags in the car and went to give him a conciliatory hug, because, really, what else could she do?

Oliver hugged her back lightly, the way you do if you still want the other person to be wrong.

I missed you, Ollie.

That's good to hear. What time do you pick Clem up?

Frank usually does it.

So what does that leave you doing all day?

I told you, I'm working.

Oh, right. Oliver looked at his watch. She noticed it was a new one.

That's a nice watch. Where'd you get it?

New boutique in SoHo. Oliver normally chose watches with much bigger faces. She knew he knew he was lying.

Oh. Althea noticed the sweat stains under his arms. Normally, she wouldn't pay any attention — it was just something that happened, like chapped lips — but now it grossed her out.

Why don't you go change? You must be hot, she said, wanting him to both fix the problem and leave her alone.

I was waiting for Coco to unpack my duffle.

Oh. How long are you staying? She meant, How long until you leave? but either question would yield the answer she wanted.

For a few weeks. I thought I would work from here for a while. She couldn't muster a *That's terrific, honey.* She was almost desperate for him to go inside, leave her alone. So she went with:

I'm sure Coco's done by now. I bet you'd like a shower. She wanted to get back in her car and drive, cry over the fact that Maze hadn't called and now she had to deal with Ollie. But she knew Oliver would never let her leave when he had just gotten there.

She followed Oliver into the house. She was going to hold it together. At least until later that night, when Oliver went to bed. She went up to her room, sat at her computer. She clicked on iTunes, opened the mix she had made. She was suddenly very tired. The roller coaster she had been on this morning — waiting for the call, picking the songs, driving to Bridge, Dylan; despair, hope, despair, hope. All over a twenty-one-year-old boy she had hired to paint her house. And what if Maze wasn't anything but that? He hadn't called her back, after all. This was a small thing — maybe he was busy — but it made her understand the desire fallacy. Before, Althea had thought the situation could be represented thus:

If X desires Y, Y desires X.
Ergo, if X calls Y, Y calls back X.

But in reality:

If X desires Y, it doesn't follow that Y desires X.
And if X calls Y, there is no certainty that Y will call back X.
In fact, the more X desires Y, the less likely Y is to desire X,
and Y will probably never, ever return a phone call from X.

So Althea was fucked. Maze had probably desired her, but only the parts of her that would appeal to any boy his age: eager mouth, arched back, damp underwear. Just someone to finish him off (though they hadn't even gotten to that) because she would and could. He was still at the point in his life when he constantly thought about sex in general — what was it, four thousand times a day? Hadn't she read that in *Cosmo*? But she actually wanted Maze himself, him specifically. Not some boy like him. Not some boy his age who was smart and had a killer body and liked to read David Foster Wallace. No, she wanted Maze. What was his appeal for her? Had she just invented him because she was lonely and needy? Or was she needy and lonely because she had invented him and he wasn't there? She wasn't sure it mattered. She felt the way she felt. But having no one tugging the other end of the rope was excruciating.

Althea decided to listen to the mix again and lie down for a little bit. She wanted to see if she could think of the songs she had picked as being nothing more than music, as having nothing to do with him. She had liked them before she met Maze. Why should her feelings for him ruin them? She would have to get someone else to finish the ceiling. She might even ask Dylan to do it. At least he could talk about Maze. Thank God she had been the one to shut it down. She plugged her headphones into the jack. Pushed play. Lay down on the couch. Maze was just a twenty-one-year-old boy who'd come to paint her house, Althea tried (really hard) to make herself believe as the first track began, but then she remembered Maze's rope belt, how she would never get to touch it again. The buttons on his oxford. Those tiny little buttons. She began again: Maze is just a twenty-one-year-old boy who came to paint . . . and then the song broke through, and Althea put her hand over her eyes and wept.

SHE WOKE UP to Coco touching her shoulder. At first, Althea thought it was Maze. But then she saw it was her housekeeper, looking concerned, and she wanted to cry all over again.

Mrs. Althea, I'm sorry to bother you, but I made lunch. I called you from the kitchen but you didn't hear. Althea wasn't sure she would ever be able to eat again. But she couldn't have Oliver come looking for her either. Oliver was not the type to ask questions, especially of her, if she went along with what was expected. So she smoothed down her dress and followed Coco to the kitchen. She'd dropped her cell phone between the cushions of the sofa. She had a new theory that Maze might be more likely to call if she wasn't checking for messages every minute. She also knew Oliver would notice if she kept looking at it. She almost never talked to anyone on the phone except him.

But when she got to the kitchen, she wished she could take Oliver's plate and throw it at the wall. He was sitting at the banquette, hunched over his computer screen, absent-mindedly eating a sandwich. Ham hung out of the toasted bread and he had crumbs and mustard on his lips. She felt sick. She had bought this food for Maze, and here was her husband eating it.

Oliver looked up at her. *Where were you? I was practically yelling.* His voice was gentle, concerned. He was no longer mad, Althea knew. When she was missing, Oliver couldn't be mad.

I fell asleep.

Were you up late? She knew he meant, Are you manic?

I've started beach walks. Wears me out.

I did notice you've lost some more weight.

It's the change in meds.

You look great. Not that you didn't before. He scooped some corn salad onto his plate. Began spearing the kernels with his fork.

Come sit, he said. *Coco unpacked the car. Thanks for getting groceries, by the way. A nice surprise.*

You're welcome, she said.

Oliver touched her shoulder, ran his fingers up to her neck. She tried her best not to flinch.

Sorry if I was a bit harsh earlier. I was hungry, which makes me insane, as you know. Oliver went back to eating. He had some corn stuck in his front teeth. She didn't bother to tell him.

She wished she could touch his elbow and say, It's fine, really, but she knew it would have come out sarcastically. Instead, she just nodded. It was all she could do not to dump the rest of his corn salad on the floor.

Aren't you going to eat? Ollie asked in his concerned voice again. *We don't want you to waste away.*

I had something earlier. In town.

Maybe just a little fruit? How about some raspberries? You love raspberries. You can't exactly skip meals, you know. And he was right. She couldn't. She had pills to take at four. But she couldn't eat those raspberries. They were supposed to be for Maze. Now she would just have to throw them away, the fragile, ripe treasures that they were.

I'll just make some toast and butter.

I'll do it.

That's okay.

No, I'll do it. Oliver's insistence on catering to her was annoying; he was acting like she might hurt herself if she used the toaster, but she had had enough fighting for the day and decided to let him do it. Oliver stood up, got the seven-grain bread, and put two slices in the toaster. After spreading them with butter and jam, he put them on the plate with the pink peonies that had a chip in it but was still her favorite.

That's perfect, Ollie. Thank you. He seemed so proud of himself. She wasn't hungry for the toast, or anything else, but she made herself eat a few bites. She gave Oliver a tiny kiss on the cheek so he wouldn't notice how little she had eaten. Ollie had turned back to his computer, and Althea got up and dumped the toast in the trash. There were crumbs from his sandwich all over the keyboard. Althea leaned over and blew on it. She decided to be nice too.

Thanks.

What are you working on?

Playing Minecraft. He laughed.

Seriously?

No. Spectacle stuff.

Show me.

You really want to know? Althea really didn't. But at least it would distract her from thinking about Maze.

Of course. If it doesn't involve graphs or Venn diagrams.

Nope. I'm the vision guy, remember? He turned the computer toward her. *These are some of the spaces we're considering for our new design studio in LA.* Oliver began to click between pictures of lofts that all looked the same to her.

Interesting. How are you going to choose?

Location. Rent. Light. Feng shui.

Feng shui? Seriously?

Not really. But I kinda like the concept of it.

Where in LA?

Not sure.

Any ideas?

Not really.

You must have some.

The creatives are looking first. Inspiration and all that. And then I go in. Why was Oliver being so indecisive? He was normally such a control freak.

Would you have to be there a lot?

At first, maybe. But after that, no, not really. More to life than work. She hoped he was there more than not. He had been home only about an hour and she already needed a break. The Maze thoughts were starting to creep back in. And instead of wanting to get away from them, she wanted to get away from Oliver and think them, no matter how painful they were.

I'm going to grab a book and read in the living room. Really, she was going to sit in the living room, check her phone, and flip through *Infinite Jest*, which sounded like a reasonable plan.

She walked up to the landing to get her book and opened the door to the room that had been hers until Ollie returned but was now, of course, once again their room, the master. Frank had put back all of the furniture. The chairs, the side tables, the dressers, the lamps, the writing desk, the rug. Coco had returned all of the frames, vases, silver trays, boxes, and books. Mr. Smiley was still there, and the ceiling was unpainted, as Oliver had pointed out, but it would eventually be done. But probably not by Maze. She couldn't bear Oliver yelling at him, treating him like staff, and chances were he wouldn't come back anyway. Sweet Maze. Gone forever.

But then she noticed the bed. She couldn't believe she hadn't taken it in when she first came in. Coco had made up the bed with the linen sheets, the down pillows, the duvet, and the cashmere throw — the things that Althea had bought that morning thinking of Maze. Althea wanted to yank them off, take them in her arms, and throw them away, but she didn't think she could touch them without breaking down.

She kicked the bed frame as hard as she could to distract herself from how she had imagined her plan going:

Maze?

Yeah?

All good?

Yup.

Should we . . .

Yup.

Anything?

Pretty much . . .

Of course, her feelings for Maze trumped radical acceptance. Her foot hurt like a bitch from kicking the bed frame, and she felt such waves of sadness in her throat, heart, and stomach, she couldn't believe she wouldn't always feel that way. She would call Coco up to the room to strip the bed. She'd tell her she'd decided the sheets didn't exactly match the new paint and would look better in the guest room. Then, eventually, she would get them from the linen closet in the middle of the night, cut them to pieces, and take them to the dump lest anyone find them. Because, really, no one else could possibly sleep on them. But before she could get Coco, Oliver walked in.

Althea, like I said, we really have to get Mark back here. It's unconscionable that someone could take advantage of you like that.

It's Maze. His name. It's Maze.

Whatever. It just pisses me off how he took advantage of you. He never would have done that if I had been there.

It's not his fault.

How's that?

I wanted to keep Mr. Smiley. Maze thought it should come off.

Mr. Smiley?

The sticker.

What?

You don't remember?

I'm sorry. Doesn't really ring a bell.

Right there. The one above the bed.

Oh. Right. I remember. Clem gave it to you to make you feel better. I didn't really want it on the ceiling but she insisted.

No, it was something you and I, that you said —

Althea, it's a sticker, I just want to —

Well, he convinced me it should go, and when he was trying to scrape it off the ceiling, he fell off his ladder and hurt his wrist. He needs to recover before he finishes.

Sounds like a scam to me. I assume he's not insured? Are you still paying him? Does he speak English? Did he say when he was coming back? Althea ignored most of Ollie's questions.

Well, I called him.

And?

I'm waiting for him to call back. That's what I'm waiting for, Ollie, more than anything. And I don't give a shit about the ceiling.

Give me his number. He'll be over here so fast your head will spin.

No. It's my project.

I'm not saying otherwise. It's not a reflection on you. Just Mike.

Jesus. It's Maze.

Well, if he doesn't call by the end of the day, we're getting someone else.

Althea felt her stomach drop. Again, there it was: him not calling.

Oliver walked across the room and kicked his shoes off, sat down on the bed.

These new sheets, however, are great. You know I love linen. He nestled back in the pillows and rolled his body around the duvet, seeking a comfortable space.

Let's lie down for a bit. Look up at the smiling face? So Maze could have scraped Smiley down for all it meant to Oliver. Had she imagined that whole story about the stupid sticker, or had he just forgotten? She wasn't sure which possibility was more depressing.

Come on, Thea, we only have about an hour before Clem comes home.

Ollie, I think I need some food. My hands are shaking. Could you make me some more toast? She hated playing the patient card when she didn't have to, but she couldn't think of any other way to get Oliver out of the bed.

You know I'm used to your hands shaking. Just come here. She felt nauseated. She didn't know what was worse, Ollie on the bed alone or her there with him. She decided it was the latter. She stalled.

Okay . . . just let me go to the bathroom.

Make it quick . . .

Althea ran her wrists under the cold water in the sink, hoping it would help her focus. She had to get him out of the bed, she just had to. Maybe it was even worth calling him into the bathroom and having sex with him there. She wasn't clear why the sheets were so important; they just were. It would serve her right if she had to have sex with Oliver in them after how she'd led Maze on during the shoot. But it just wasn't possible. She might throw up or stay so dry she'd bleed.

There had to be a way around it. Maybe she could tell him that she had her period? (He would notice that there wasn't any evidence.) That she had a urinary tract infection? (That wouldn't affect him and he might not be sympathetic.) That she expected a call from an art dealer any minute? (Even though he would find this implausible, he would keep that to himself and tell her she could certainly call whoever it was back after they were done.) Or maybe — bingo! — she could tell him she had missed a few birth control pills, and they certainly didn't want to risk her getting pregnant. (He couldn't very well admit he carried condoms.)

Althea . . . everything all right? Ollie's tone had changed. He was still waiting, but he no longer sounded as eager.

Sorry. Something I ate just didn't agree with me, Althea yelled back. Maybe that will work, she thought. Who wants to sleep with that? Gross. *Do you want me to take a shower?*

No . . . you're just fine. Again, his impatience seemed to have vanished. Did he really want to go through with it? She had convinced herself by this point that she would walk into the bedroom and find Oliver reading some paper or maybe a book. He might even be out of the bed and sitting on the chaise longue, which he swore had the best light. But Oliver hadn't moved. At least, not really.

When Althea came into the bedroom, the first thing she noticed was that the clothes Ollie had been wearing minutes before were now folded carefully on the bench at the end of the bed with his new watch on top. And then, there it was.

Oliver was completely naked, his head tilted back in the down pillows, his eyes half closed. His legs were spread, his knees bent, and the soles of his feet were together. His hand was on his penis, and he was stroking himself. She wanted to throw up. Oliver looked at her and began moving his foreskin up and down more quickly.

Thought I would get started, time and all . . . Oliver could barely speak.

She could hardly breathe. Was watching her husband masturbate on Maze's sheets literally going to kill her? At least Oliver seemed to forget she was there, didn't expect her to join him. He kept at it, his eyes going so glassy it looked like he couldn't see anymore. Then Oliver scrunched up his whole face, clenched his jaw, got that pained look that she knew meant one thing. It would be seconds before he *got there*, before Oliver came. She needed to stop him, so she screamed:

GET OUT! OF MY BED! Oliver sat up. She watched as his penis went limp. He almost lunged at her but grabbed at his hair instead.

What the fuck?

Get the hell out of my bed!

Your bed? It's mine too. Last I checked. He crawled to the end of the bed, grabbed the pile of clothes from the bench, and started to get dressed.

Get out!

Althea. Stop yelling. What's going on? If you only knew, Oliver. She watched as he finished getting dressed and stood up.

It calmed her down a bit.

Oliver. I buy new sheets and I don't even get to sleep in them before you're masturbating on them.

I'm excited to see you. It's clear you were trying to avoid the whole thing. Just because you can't doesn't mean I shouldn't.

Actually, turns out I can.

Did you have a week free or something?

No, took about four minutes.

Wow. What's the secret?

I guess my hand has more patience than you do.

You're acting weird. Are you feeling racy?

No. Are you?

You buy food. Probably four thousand dollars' worth of bedding. You're not eating, you yell at me for jacking off in our bed, and supposedly you're having orgasms now after I don't know how many years.

You'd be surprised but many women shop, diet, fight with their husbands, and masturbate.

Sure. But not you.

Well, thank God you came home when you did. I clearly need to be supervised.

And I saw Lola in the kitchen. How many times have you had her over to sit for Clem?

I've been working. I've been setting up bogus shoots with twenty-one-year-old boys because I can't think of any other way to spend time alone with them.

So you've said. But that wasn't my question.

A few days a week.

Define a few.

I don't know — two, three.

So that would be five, six.

Something like that.

So let's just say seven. Seven days a week. And what did Clem have for dinner last night?

How should I know? I told you, I've been working.

What's she been reading?

Moby-Dick.

Sure, that's ongoing. But what else?

You got me.

Well, last time I talked to her, she had just started Catcher in the Rye.

I don't hover, Ollie.

Okay, where's her camp?

Stop with the quiz, okay? But fine. It's off 27. She was safe with this one; practically everything in East Hampton was off Route 27.

What's the name of her favorite horse?

Cut it out. You know Clem's not sentimental like that. She probably doesn't have one.

Yes, she does. Nutmeg.

Oliver, just because you're good at conversation and get the tiny details doesn't mean you're a better parent. Well, actually, she thought, it probably does.

Have you even seen her — I mean, spent any real time with her — in the past month?

No, she hadn't, Althea had to admit, not to Oliver, but to herself. At least she owned it. She hadn't tried and failed with Clem. She just hadn't even tried.

Well, Clem kind of made horse camp her priority, she said. *You know how she is. She really didn't want to spend any time with me.*

Wow. You expect me to believe that bullshit? She's ten, not seventeen, Althea. Could you possibly think about something besides work?

But Oliver, I have. I have been thinking about Maze. Maze, who came to paint our house, reads David Foster Wallace, and has a scar on his biceps that drives me crazy. As for Clem, there will be plenty of time for her later. Just not this summer.

I could ask you the same question, Oliver. What exactly have you been doing for the past month?

Working my ass off. He started rubbing his nose. He always touched his nose when he lied.

With Claire?

Yes, with Claire. Among others.

But especially with Claire.

No, not especially with Claire. She's only one person out of a whole team.

How's the pregnancy going? Did she announce the father yet?

She's still keeping it pretty close to the chest.

Maybe there are several candidates?

Althea, maybe you need a nap.

I had one. Before lunch, remember? But I bet you know who it is.

Why would you say that? He pulled on his nose again.

Just a guess. Hey, can I see your watch? Oliver had already put it back on, and when she asked, he covered its face with his hand, as if to make it disappear.

Why?

I'm your wife. I like it. I think I want to wear it.

I've got plenty of others. This one is kind of junky. I bought it for the beach.

What's the big deal?

Althea, I don't know what game you are playing, but stop it —

Well, if you don't let me see it, I will tell Coco to change the duvet because Mr. Oliver got semen on it when he was . . .

well . . . It was a stupid thing, but Althea knew Oliver hated being embarrassed in front of *service providers* almost more than anything else.

That's pretty mature of you. But he unbuckled the watch and handed it to Althea. She flipped it to the back.

There Althea found exactly what she was looking for: an inscription. It was discreet, but it still said everything Althea suspected or, really, already knew: *Trois.*

Trois. Mommy and Daddy, and Baby makes three. *Trois* would fit nicely on a license plate. Oliver could certainly make up any number of explanations for it, but she knew. Oliver had come home to test-drive her for the last time, to prove to both of them that it was over, that there was nothing left between them.

Congratulations, Papa. Althea said calmly. *Boy or girl?*

Althea, you have to understand —

No, I don't.

Claire —

Has great nipples —

This isn't funny.

You invite Claire to our house, and I fire her when she comes on to you. Then she throws the shitty ice cream maker she gave me as a house present at my head, and you get upset with me and leave with her. I think that's pretty hysterical.

Althea. I'm not done —

I think you are.

Althea, seriously. Sit down. Listen to me. I've thought a lot about this. She sat down on the bed. He looked more nervous than she had ever seen him. She liked it. For once, he was admitting he had fucked up. She tried to figure out whether it would be more satisfying to yell or give him the silent treatment.

I was never dating Claire, per se. There was just one incident . . . She loved how clinical Ollie was about discussing sexual matters.

I tried to talk her into having it terminated, but she refused. I told her I would help her financially and be as supportive as I could, and we would be friends no matter what. Althea really didn't want to hear the backstory. It did hurt to hear it after all. She grabbed Oliver's hand and squeezed it, as if to bring him back to the present.

Then she came to work on the house. That day on the beach, she started talking about the baby like it had nothing to do with me. All of a sudden, my feelings changed and I wanted to be part of it. I wanted to go through with the whole thing. Remember I never got to before . . .

Of course she remembered.

We spent almost every minute together in the city. That's when she bought me the watch. And she told me she loved me. It was the first time she had ever said it to anyone, apparently. She said she'd been waiting to make sure I was completely committed to her.

Oliver tossed the words off with the insouciance of *hello* or *goodbye.* Committed? It seemed to her that the only time Oliver was committed to her was when she had to be carted off to New York–Pres.

Claire started to talk about moving to France together. Wanted me to meet her mother. She was open to having Clem come with us.

Althea began to wish she had spent more time with Clem that summer. She really couldn't imagine being alone, not having the two of them. She started to cry. What else could she do? Oliver surprised her by not hugging her. It was as if he was afraid he would not get to the end of the story.

We were talking about getting married. Claire said divorce would be good for both you and me in the end. That your illness wasn't my problem. That it was time for me to have my own life. And for you too. The thought of Claire discussing her illness, dissecting their marriage, did more than help Althea regain her composure; it made her furious.

And what did you say to that, Oliver?

Nothing.

You said nothing?

Well, nothing else about you.

So then, after that discussion about what a bloodsucking head case I was, you guys . . . fucked . . .

No. Don't be ridiculous.

Ollie, just get to the point.

I realized Claire was wrong. I wasn't unhappy with you.

Oh, thanks. But you'd be happier with her.

Maybe. No. But it doesn't matter. I still love you. I love Clem. I don't need to start over.

So why are you wearing that ridiculous watch?

She begged me not to take it off. Said it would make my leaving easier on her. Knowing I had it.

Are you an idiot? She wanted me to know.

I would have told you anyway, Althea. But you're missing the point. I'm choosing you.

Over Claire? I'm your wife. I shouldn't have to be chosen.

And just then, Althea realized that despite everything Oliver had done for her and all the years they had spent together — she didn't want him back.

Ollie, I can't do this. You're going to have to leave.

Althea, you don't mean that. You can't. You need me.

I'm not saying I don't. But this is too much. You can't really expect me to let you come back after you got another woman pregnant and considered marrying her. So, yes, I do mean it. You have to go. I'd rather risk being alone.

I can't let you do that, Althea.

You don't have to let me.

If I leave, I'm not coming back. Do you hear me? No matter what you do, I'm not coming back.

Now you're threatening me? Go back to the city and take Clem with you. Let's make something up to explain it and spare her the drama for the time being. Lola can send her clothes. I need some time alone.

You know where time alone gets you? Neck in a noose. Then New York–Presbyterian.

I'm not going to kill myself, Oliver. That's not what this is about.

Actually, I'll give that to you. You never actually succeed, Althea. There's just a whole lot of trying. And that's the bullshit.

I don't point the gun at my head when my husband impregnates and falls in love with a beautiful Frenchwoman and spares me none of the details, Althea thought. I point the gun at my head when my brain turns to a lump of gray clay and I am left stranded in an incomprehensible reality that I can't navigate. Where I stare at my cell phone, too bewildered by its mechanics to make a phone call, send a text, or even turn it on. Where, no matter how many times I ask people, I can't remember what day comes after Tuesday. Where I eat soup with a fork because there is meat in it, and even though each time I spill it all over myself, I keep at it, thinking the next time it will work, it must. If Oliver doesn't know this by now, doesn't understand this, then he doesn't know or understand me, Althea thought.

He wasn't leaving her; he was leaving his idea of her. And he wasn't ruining her life; he was ruining his idea of her life.

Oliver stomped to the closet, grabbed his suitcase, threw it on the bed. He began stuffing it with shirts, pants, ties, boxer shorts, not even bothering to fold them. His loafers, running shoes, flip-flops. She wondered when he was going to wear these, but she was grateful she wouldn't have to look at them. Then:

Where are my orange Crocs? Where the hell are my orange Crocs?

I don't know.

They were here when I left.

I didn't touch them.

They didn't walk away by themselves. Althea hated those orange Crocs. Plastic clogs with holes in them. She probably would have thrown them out along with Claire's button if she'd thought of it.

Maybe you left them in the city.

I didn't take them to the city. They don't wear Crocs in the city.

Men don't really wear Crocs here either —

Fuck you, Althea. I'm not leaving without my Crocs.

Check the mudroom.

I never leave them there.

Well, I can't help you. Sorry.

I told you, I'm not leaving until I find them. He sat down on the bed, folded his arms, pouted like a child.

Let me look. She went into the closet. Dug around. They were shoved way back by his tennis shoes.

Here you go. Oliver took them from her. Threw them against the wall.

AFTER OLIVER LEFT, she felt very calm. Steady. She had just told her husband of sixteen years, the man who had always come back to get her from behind some locked door or other, to leave, to go fuck himself.

The house was empty. Althea could hear the silence. She wondered if Oliver would worry about her, change his mind and come back. She thought about calling him to say she was okay. But she didn't want to talk to him; she just wanted to keep him from coming to check on her.

When had Claire gotten pregnant? Obviously before she came to stay at the house. She remembered the tiny roll of fat visible when she was in her bikini. Yes, Claire was already pregnant when Oliver asked her to work on the house. Was that why he had asked her? When had the *incident*, as Ollie put it, happened? Did it really matter? But Claire was much older than the babies Oliver usually liked. Was Claire's face enough for him? And why did she choose Oliver? She could have had anyone she wanted.

Althea felt her bra digging into her back and took it off, threw it down by her feet. It drove Oliver crazy when she left clothes anywhere but the hamper, but now he wasn't there to snap at her. She could take her clothes off all over the house if she wanted to.

When she went into the kitchen to look for her car keys, she realized she was hungry. She opened the fridge and it was empty except for a few grapefruits, which she didn't have the energy or concentration to peel. She always ate them this way, like oranges. She almost regretted telling Coco to empty it of all of the fruit and cheese and corn salad and pie but then remembered her heartbreak watching Oliver eating that sandwich and knew she wouldn't have been able to stomach those things anyway. She opened a cabinet and saw some of Oliver's Grape-Nuts, which she hated, and Clem's Lucky Charms, which made her sad, since Oliver was right, she had gotten absolutely nowhere with Clem this summer. On the next shelf were condiments, which of course she couldn't eat, but on the top, pushed to the back, she found a huge bag of jumbo marshmallows, long wooden skewers, and a box of giant Hershey bars.

The summer before, Oliver had had the idea that they should go to Atlantic Beach and make s'mores after dinner one night. They would build a fire, bring chairs and music. Althea had been out of her mind with the Visions and had decided to go topless. But she had not announced this until they got to the parking lot, and when Ollie tried to stop her it became a scene.

The summer girl, Mina, walked Clem down to the beach to distract her, but it was dark and chilly, and Clem lay down in the sand and wouldn't get up. Oliver finally got Althea to put a shirt on, but then she said she wanted to go to Talkhouse instead of sitting around in the sand toasting the marshmallows and eating them, which, in her opinion, just wasn't sexy. Oliver told her no, and she told him she was a grown woman and could do whatever she wanted and began soliciting rides from other people in the lot. He had no choice but to tell her he would take her after all, and he rounded up Clem and Mina and they all drove to Talkhouse and dropped her off. Oliver came back for her and found her dancing on the stage with the Whalers, shoes off, feet filthy, spilling Perrier all over. So there were no s'mores that night, or any night since then. There were only the ingredients Oliver had bought by himself at Waldbaum's, thinking it might be something fun for them to do as a family.

Althea pulled it all down on the kitchen counter. She felt like kneading the marshmallows together into a sugary loaf. But they were hard and stale and she knew they wouldn't coalesce. She picked up a wooden skewer. The point was sharp. Just sharp enough that it would have been confiscated if she'd tried to take it into the hospital or hidden by Ollie when she was released. But here she was, holding it, with no one to say no. She could poke herself in the eye or the throat if she wanted to. But she didn't want to. For now, the long stick was just another example of something her family hadn't been able to do because of her. *Yay!*

She put the marshmallows and the sticks in a paper grocery bag she found under the sink. She couldn't exactly give them away, but they were a bitter memory in the house. She added the pack of stickers to the bag and hoisted it onto her hip. She pulled open a drawer to grab some scissors in case she decided to open the marshmallows when she was getting rid of them. She didn't want to rip open the plastic bag with her teeth like some kind of feral dog. Then she saw them. Or saw them again: Claire's cigarettes. She must have put them back in the drawer. There was no getting rid of them. Unless. She went upstairs to get her camera.

It took her ten minutes to drive to Atlantic Beach. There was still enough light for her to work. She didn't bother to change into her uniform of cutoff jeans and a T-shirt, just kept on her sundress and flip-flops from earlier. She hadn't even put her bra back on. She worried that if people saw her wearing this, they would think she wasn't a professional, that she was just someone messing around with an expensive camera, but she was in such a hurry to get there and set up, she told herself that even if someone was looking at her, it didn't really matter. This was the first time she had done a shoot without anyone else, and since she had the movement of the ocean to deal with, it was going to be hard enough as it was.

Althea had not been back to Atlantic Beach since the s'mores episode the summer before. She always told Ollie that coming out of the Visions was like waking up from a blackout, to escape responsibility, but of course she remembered them. Or some parts of them. The night of the s'mores, of course. But that was just one. There were so many others. As always with her, there were plenty of examples of plain old crazy. Tonight, though, she didn't feel crazy. She felt like a woman at the beach with a camera. Melancholic, maybe, because her husband was gone and she maybe loved this boy who was, well, so many things to her, but who was also not here now and probably would never be.

Althea looked at the sand and the waves and the sun that hovered in the sky. She kicked off her flip-flops and walked with the grocery bag and her camera toward the water.

She took out the sticks, the marshmallows, and the stickers and set them down in the sand. She speared a marshmallow with a stick and put a Mr. Smiley sticker on the marshmallow, like a face. She assembled five of them. Then she stuck the sticks in the wet sand like they were scarecrows, just by the shore break, where the waves could hit and gently nudge them. She lay down on her stomach and began to shoot. In her head, she talked to her husband:

The project is called the Water Experiment. I want to know, will the waves hit all the sticks with the same force? With the same regularity? Or, rather, big picture: What makes someone go under? What keeps someone in the game?

Althea took pictures for an hour, until the sun was setting. The marshmallows were almost dissolved by the water, and most of the stickers had come unstuck, but all the sticks except one were still firmly planted in the sand. Which one? Althea got to choose. It wasn't really an experiment, after all. Just Althea working something out. She wasn't a scientist. She was a photographer. She got to arrange things as she wanted.

So, who was knocked down by her Water Experiment? It wasn't Clem, obviously. Clem had survived having Althea as a mother so far. She had made it one, two, three . . . ten years. Was it her? No, she might fall, but she always got up. What about Oliver? Had she knocked him down? Did he need to be the one who cleaned up the blood, gave the meds, packed the duffle, even though he had a *thing* with Claire? Or was it Claire who'd fallen? Or Maze? Would something knock Maze down? And who would find him, help him get up?

She knew someone had gotten pushed down by the water, but please, God, not him. Althea felt like she had to do something, so she threw a handful of sand into the ocean. There was nothing to see when it landed; a wave just absorbed the sand, but Althea felt better for the gesture. She collected the sticks, threw them in the garbage, and walked back to her car.

Her whole body was damp and covered with sand; it was on her face, her arms, in her hair. Her thin dress was almost transparent, soaked from her lying on the beach as she shot the photos. She was hungry and felt like ice cream. She checked her phone. No calls. She shut it off. Now she thought about nothing but how the frozen milk and sugar with bits of cookie dough would taste in her mouth. But first she would go home and change.

Althea pulled the car into the driveway and walked carefully through the darkness to the front door, trying hard not to trip in her flip-flops. She hadn't remembered to turn on the outside lights, and when she got closer, she saw a figure sitting on the front step. Her first thought was that Oliver had come back and was waiting for her like he had been that morning. But Oliver would have turned on the porch light, at the very least. She should have been wary, but really, she knew all along who it was.

Maze. Althea was about to cry after all that waiting.

Want some? There was a cardboard box from Sam's Pizza sitting next to him. Maze held out a slice.

Maybe later. He carefully put the slice back in the box, wiped his hands on his T-shirt, and looked up at her. He was wearing his GREEN shirt and the same cords he'd had on the night of the shoot.

Got your message.

You know, Maze, most people just call back.

Yeah, well. I'm not really a phone person. What's up?

She didn't know how to start. She just wanted to sit next to him, breathing. And she knew this would be fine with Maze. After a long pause, she said:

It's so hot, Maze. Why are you wearing pants?

Dunno. I always wear them. Unless I'm in the water.

So I've noticed.

You know, I like your dress, Maze said.

She looked down. Her sundress was still wet from the beach, and her nipples were erect and visible through the fabric. She wasn't sure if he was teasing her or if she was teasing him. Probably both. She crossed her arms over her chest.

I've had it forever. I was just at the beach. Taking pictures.

Of what? Maze scratched his ankle.

Of marshmallows.

Huh?

It's complicated. It's absurd, she thought. Marshmallows? With stickers on them?

So, what's up? You said you wanted me to do something?

Just this, Maze. Just don't let me be stupid enough to send you away again. *Right. I did.*

What is it?

The ceiling. I want you to finish it. Maze laughed and picked up another slice of pizza.

It was always pretty obvious you did, he said.

Well, sometimes I can be weird about stuff, I'm sorry. But I really do. Want you to.

But you can't change your mind this time.

I won't. Promise.

Maze put down his pizza. Looked at her. Not just in her general direction, but right at her. She looked back. She couldn't see the color of his eyes in the dimness (of course, she knew they were brown, like hers; darker, but still brown), but she could feel them on her. She could feel him sitting next to her, even though they weren't touching, not even a little bit. But her nipples, her braless nipples, were still bound up by her sundress, rubbing against it, trying to break free. And even though Maze was sitting right there looking at her, and she was looking back, these nipples under her wet sundress had become almost unbearable; really, they were driving her crazy. She was sure they had doubled in size. Her face flushed so hot it felt like someone had slapped her. And down between her legs — well, there was nothing to say.

She had gotten distracted by all this; she should have been thinking about what to say to him (she'd thought of things she would never say, of course, like Just don't go away ever again; I really don't care about the fucking ceilings, you know, just take off this stupid dress). So Althea uncrossed her arms and took her hands away from her chest and reached up and touched Maze's face. She let her fingers roam around his eyelids, cheeks, nose, mouth, jawbone, hairline. But after ten seconds (or was it eight, seven? She really couldn't say), Maze stopped her, gathered up her fingers, lightly pulled her hands away, and put them down in her lap.

She was sure now that Maze was going to take his turn — touch her with his long fingers, his callused palms, his smooth nails that were always carefully trimmed. She thought, I want him to touch my chest right now, right below my neck, rub off the salt and sand. I want Maze to touch my —

But then, before she could finish the thought, Maze put one hand on the back of her neck, cupped her chin with the other, and pulled her in for a kiss.

It wasn't a *famishing*, with all of Maze behind it, him grabbing her chin, biting her lips, pulling the back of her head toward him, then tilting his head to the side, putting his tongue into her mouth, seeking out her tongue, without concern for air.

No, it was a *soft kiss*, a whisper, Maze's assurance to her that they were not in a hurry; his promise to her that they had hours and hours to do whatever they wanted to do to each other. They could afford to go from tender to passionate and back again. She loved kissing Maze, she absolutely loved kissing him; it made her feel high.

While Maze was gently kissing her, she put her hands underneath his GREEN T-shirt and walked them up his back. The cotton was damp against his skin and Althea wished she could kiss him there, smell his sweat. But of course she couldn't stop kissing Maze's mouth. They had gotten into a rhythm, pressing into each other gently, sucking, but not hard, taking one breath together instead of two. So she moved her hands up to his shoulders, began massaging them, back and forth, like she was trying to push him away just for the pleasure of pulling him into her again. She moved down his ribs, spreading her fingers out over them, gently framing the bones, as if they might break. Then she got to his stomach — it was hard and flat; she thought of all the laps in the pool those muscles represented — and traced the soft trail of hair that went from his navel to just below the waist of his cords.

She didn't want to just drop their kissing, break it — it was so beautiful, really — so she crawled into Maze's lap, wrapped her legs around his back, and started hard-kissing him. He met the new intensity instantly, as if he had been waiting for it. Sitting on top of Maze, she could feel it, could feel him, hard beneath his cords. But this time, she knew he wasn't giving her permission to go farther. She already had it.

Maze tugged at the straps of her sundress as if the straps would know what he wanted and magically come off. But they crossed below the shoulders and buttoned in the back. He tried sliding them down her arms, but they got tangled around her elbows. Instead of ripping the straps apart and ruining the buttons (Althea was going to tell him to just do it, she couldn't wait. She'd throw the fucking dress away), Maze carefully lifted her up off his lap. He turned her to the side, slowly undid the buttons, uncrossed the straps, slid the dress to her waist. She couldn't believe he was able to focus on such details. Her body needed to be touching his, needed to be touched by his, constantly, right now. But that was Maze. She knew it was just Maze being Maze.

He took her onto his lap again, facing him. He put one hand on her lower back, the other behind her neck, and slowly tilted her away from him, just a little bit. Then paused. She felt like she was at the top of a roller coaster about to drop. She could feel the warm night air on her naked chest, still sprinkled with sand. She could see her nipples and breasts, finally freed from the damp sundress, but they were now so big it was outrageous. Maze had to touch them, *Please, Maze, please*, or she was going to lose her mind. Really. She looked at her legs, her dress bunched just above her knees. Their hips were still pressed together; she was rocking back and forth into him. Maze was so hard now it was difficult to believe his erection was just blood and flesh and not some kind of weapon. But there was still the pause. Please, Maze, please. Althea tried to whisper this, but the only thing she managed was a small moan.

But she knew, looking back on it later, there hadn't really been a pause. Or he hadn't meant anything by it. Maze was just looking at her face or the sky or who knows what for one more second. Because Maze didn't rush. He got the job done, always, but he never rushed. And so, just as Althea, sundress around her waist, was ready to sit up, remove his hands from where he had carefully placed them on her body, and yank off his rope belt, Maze leaned forward and bit her lip. Then, gently, methodically, he brushed some sand off her cheek, worked his way down her neck, worked his way down to her breast. He took her nipple in his mouth and began to suck on it, gently biting her, teasing her. It was tenderness unadulterated. *Tender* was the place where you hurt, the place that left you vulnerable. But *tender* was also the person you could expose your wounds to without fear of further attack.

But who was the vulnerable one? Was it Althea, who was half naked, her whole body flushed and shaking because she wanted this boy so much? She, who had let him — no, had *begged* him — to put his mouth on her and who now was about to cry, it felt so unbearably good? Or was it Maze? Maze, whose erection jabbed at her through his soft cords, an erection hard and fierce but really, like all others, just a manifestation of his need and want? Both, she thought. They were both vulnerable. And they were both going to — no, not take care of each other, that wasn't what was happening here. They were going to not make things worse.

Maze lifted his head from her chest and pulled her upright, into his own chest. He leaned into her neck, began kissing and sucking on it, softly and then with more force. Her hands gripped Maze's T-shirt. She had to take it off. She had to get the fucking thing off. She pulled his head away from her neck, grabbed his shirt at the waist, and yanked it up and off him. She had to see it again. Absolutely needed to see it. The scar on Maze's right biceps.

Of course, she knew exactly where it was, even in the dark. She started at his shoulder and slowly ran her hand down his arm, drawing out the approach as long as possible. When she got to the scar, she traced it gently with her fingers, as if the skin were still just healing. She leaned in and pressed her cheek against it, and Maze began to stroke her hair. Then she turned her head and just hovered over it, breathing. She was so still; it was almost impossible to be as still as she was. But what was coming was so exquisite that Althea forced herself to wait just a little longer. She was swollen and throbbing beneath her underwear; her cheeks were flushed and burning, and she practically had to bite her tongue to keep herself from crying out. But she was still.

And then. At last. She leaned in close to the scar and kissed it. Just once, right on the top edge. A very precise kiss. For so long, she had wanted exactly this. To kiss Maze's scar. Caused by a cut he hadn't bothered to get stitched up. And now she had done it. When she released his arm, she was in a state of bliss. She reached for Maze's bare shoulders, pressed her face right up against his. Her whole body shuddered.

Maze. Just saying his name was almost as intense as touching him.

Mmm? He was busy kissing her under the chin.

Maze . . . She was really too far gone to talk, but she wanted to tell him something, she wasn't sure what, but something, before they kept going.

Mm-hm?

Maze. She still didn't know.

Yeah? He stopped kissing her and pressed his forehead to hers. She wanted something big and important to come to her, but nothing did. Her mouth was just to the side of his and she was desperate to kiss him again.

Do you think you could get around to finishing that ceiling?
On it.

Maze lifted her up off his lap and stood. He scooped her up in his arms and carried her around to the back of the pool house. There was no more being still now; it was everything she could do not to squirm. Maze walked quickly and held her tightly, and she curled into his warm, beautiful torso. He put her down by the outside shower.

He turned the water on and ran his fingers under it, waited. But she couldn't and she leaned down and pulled at the knot of his belt. She tugged his cords down to his ankles and pressed her face into the blue cotton of his boxers, running her cheek over his erection, which was now so swollen she was amazed he could still walk. She was overcome by how much she now wanted — no, *needed* — to touch Maze there; she felt like she would not be able to breathe again until she did. She was about to reach into his boxers and . . . well, she didn't know what she was going to do, exactly, but she had to do something; he was so hard and her desire for him was such that she wanted to have all of him everywhere at once, and there was also the tenderness that made her think of Maze waiting, Maze waiting for her to take him there, to that place where his mind emptied out and there was just the sweet release, like waves breaking and dissolving into the sandy shore.

She didn't want Maze to wait; he was ready to get there, she knew, so she was about to reach for him, but he pulled her hand away and guided her into the shower. She was still half wearing her dress.

Maze took off his pants, left his boxers on, and got in the shower with Althea. He turned her around so she was facing the wall and then stood behind her, looping his arm around the front of her waist. He reached under her arm and pressed it lightly against her breastbone. The soap felt hard and smooth, like a rock he had just picked up. But as Maze began to slide it back and forth over her chest, up and around her nipples and the contours of her breasts, the once-solid bar dissolved into sudsy ribbons. Althea put her hand on top of Maze's and guided it over her ribs, over and around her stomach, back and forth between her hipbones. Now the soap was so slippery under the hot water that their hands, one on top of the other, were able to easily trace shapes with it: a sideways figure eight on her lower stomach, a cross up and over her chest.

Maze told her to bend over, then he took her by the waist

and lifted her wet sundress up onto her back. He pulled down her underwear, slid two fingers inside her, then three. Once again, she put her hand over his and put two of her fingers inside herself to join his. At first their strokes were slow but deep, and Althea felt herself softening, opening up. Then they sped up, and her breath became ragged, as if it just couldn't make it down her throat. Then Maze. Maze began rolling her clitoris in tiny circles with his thumb. Now she was almost completely wrecked; her body was about to give in, surrender, *come*, whether she wanted it to or not. But she was not ready. She didn't want to succumb by herself, leave Maze behind.

She lifted his hands away, stood up, and watched as he casually sucked on the index finger that had been inside her. She turned the showerhead to the side, slid her hands inside the elastic of his boxers, pulled them carefully down to his ankles. She knelt in front of him like she was praying and gently lined the trail of dark hair that connected his navel to that sweet area just below his hipbones with soft, gentle kisses. Maze fell back against the wall but did not grab her head or pull her into him. She massaged his legs, taut with muscle, starting, as Maze would do, at the top, with his upper quads, and stopping only when she got to his ankles. His ankles. She leaned over and started licking one of his anklebones, then sucking on it, gripping his heel to steady herself. While Maze did not seem at all destabilized by her pace and the stops she was making on his body (his knees were bent and his arms were loose), Althea was getting frantic.

She looked up at Maze. His eyes were closed, as if he were in some kind of trance. She sat up, got on her knees again. While Maze might have looked dreamy, far away, really, he was not. It was all right there; she could feel the unbearable tension of longing in his erection. Finally, it was undeniable, Maze couldn't put it off any longer — he had to take something for himself.

She wrapped her fingers around the base of his penis and cupped the soft pouch of flesh that hung underneath it. She slid his skin up and back for a minute before nuzzling him with her face. She dipped her tongue into the slit at the top, tasting the salty fluid pooling there. She closed her lips around him and began sucking. Then Althea heard him. Finally, she heard him.

Oh God, Maze whispered. *Oh my God.*

She kept going. Maze slid down the wall a bit and put his hands on the back of her head, applying just enough pressure to let her know he absolutely needed her there, that she couldn't possibly go away.

She felt him grow bigger in her mouth. He started thrusting his hips, making himself go deeper, down into her throat, as if he couldn't stand to have anything, even air, between them.

She kept going. Maze moved his hands slightly forward so he was holding the back of her neck and his palms were on her face. She could feel him shaking. She knew it would be any second now . . .

But then Maze said, he actually said:

Stop.

She sat back. She felt like Maze had pushed her down a steep hill. She stood up, planning to smack him (she had to do something), but then she saw his face. His cheeks were flushed and his eyes were glazed and she could hear his breathing, which was as quick as if he had just finished a heat. But somehow, he was still able to lean into her and very slowly and deliberately kiss her gently on the mouth. His lips met hers with such force, his tongue found hers with such precision, and their mouths moved together in such synchronicity that Althea almost passed out.

But then Maze put one hand behind her back and one under her knees and once again lifted her up forcefully and started carrying her as if she couldn't walk (though at this point, Althea was pretty sure she couldn't). But why didn't they just stay there, keep going? Althea had finally gotten to kiss all the places, all of them, on the boy she loved, this time not having to temper her urgency; she'd gotten to bite his lips and suck on his scar. She was on the verge of coming her head off, right back in the shower again. She was so close she felt the contractions approaching, the wave about to hit. And she knew Maze was at that same place; she could hear it in his breathing. Would they get wherever he was taking them before they both lost their momentum? She almost told him to stop, that things were perfect as they were, but then she realized Maze must have a plan and knew there was no telling him what to do. Maze was the most stubborn person she had ever met. She would just have to try and hold herself back. She had waited so long for him, after all.

Maze laid her down on the grass not far from the pool, pulled her wet sundress down her legs and tossed it on a chaise nearby. It was completely dark except for the moon. This time, there was no music, no mixes. She certainly didn't care anymore. This was so much better, the two of them together in a silence broken only by the uncensored sounds of each other.

Maze straddled her hips, leaned over her, and began stroking her wet hair, fanning it out carefully in the grass. She could feel his penis pressing into her stomach. She wanted to scream; she could barely stand it anymore. Really, she thought it would have felt better if he had slapped her; the tension was driving her insane.

He untangled Althea's fingers from his hair and put his face directly next to hers. So close that she could see his eyelashes (or she swore she could, even the dark). And finally, Maze reached down and gently slid himself inside her. When they got to the end, she felt so high from it she wanted to laugh, just smile and laugh. Was this what they called ecstasy? Bliss? She finally understood why Maze had taken his time, drawn things out.

Then Althea really wanted to try something else. She whispered to Maze.

That's cool with me.

Althea didn't want to ask him if it really was, but still . . . He flipped over.

She put her hands on his shoulders and pulled him into her, took her time to sit straight on top of him. It was a position she had avoided since she had first gotten ill, but when she was in college and before, she had loved it.

Later, Althea had been embarrassed by all the weight the meds had made her gain, the impatient look on Oliver's face waiting for it to be over — he couldn't exactly tell her they had been at it thirty minutes and the sight of her stomach just wasn't doing it for him. And now? She was thinner and off the meds that stopped her from coming, but really, as much as she trusted Maze, he was twenty-one and she was seventeen years older. What would he think? But then, suddenly, she didn't care. She was ready to try again. She looked down.

Maze had his hands on her hips and a half smile on his face, and he was watching her intently like she was the most amazing thing he had ever seen. Like wasn't this an excellent idea.

Then Althea — she couldn't believe it, but she began stroking herself while Maze was inside her. At first, Althea thought she was doing it for Maze, that it was the kind of porno-chick move a twenty-one-year-old would be into, but then she realized that that wasn't it. She was just going for it, not really thinking about Maze at all. Althea closed her eyes when she was getting close. She didn't want to share this moment. She wanted it all for herself.

But still, a few seconds later, when Althea came so hard that she felt like her entire body, including her mind and all its bothersome thoughts, had been emptied out, she understood that it had been a mutual endeavor. Something this intense couldn't be one-sided. Maybe later, yes, memories would shift and one of them would remember one thing or another. One memory might be painful, and the other not, but that wasn't really the point, was it? For that moment, she and Maze had shared an intimacy.

ALTHEA FELL INTO Maze and put her head on his chest. After all that, she had a heightened sense of his smell and it was utterly soporific. She felt like sleeping beside him forever.

That was amazing, she said.

Yep.

How could you possibly know how to do that?

WikiHow.

Seriously.

I dunno. Practice.

You're twenty-one.

Didn't bother you before.

And what about me? Does the fact that I'm eighty bother you?

Nope.

Althea slid over a bit, began touching his scar. As much as she had loved the earlier urgency, she was relieved they were now exhausted enough to talk.

Maze, your scar . . . you know I'm obsessed with it.

Sorta obvious.

Do you think that's kind of weird?

Kind of?

You know, the first time I saw it . . .

Okay. Creepy.

Althea hit him in the arm.

Ow.

Althea kissed his temple. *Kidding.* Though of course she wasn't.

Maze?

Yeah?

Can I ask you something?

As long as it's not about the scar, sure.

Were you mad about the last time? When I couldn't . . .

Nah. I knew it'd happen eventually.

Really? How?

Dunno. Just did.

Why? I mean, why me?

Because.

That's it? Because?

Well, I guess I thought you were interesting.

And what about now —

Still do. I don't want to sound like a dick, but could you move over? My arm's falling asleep.

Sure. But by now, I mean how do you feel about me now? Do you think we will see each other again?

Why's it up to me? Aren't you the grownup here?

Stop it.

Do you really think it would even be good a second time?

Why wouldn't it?

Look. Can't we chill out and enjoy what we just did?

How? It's already over.

Maybe. But it was excellent. And we will always be friends.

That's just great. Really.

I don't have many friends, you know.

She turned away from him and started rubbing her eyes.

Hey, there's nothing wrong here.

She laughed, just a little, and allowed herself to lie next to him and not cry. And Maze, the true friend that he was, let her.

OLIVER CALLED a week after he'd left. She was surprised it had taken him so long. Anyone who wasn't his wife would have thought he sounded cheery on the other end of the phone, but she could tell he was faking it. She let him ask her how she was.

Fine, really. Just fine. And you?

No, seriously. You can tell me if you're not. I thought you might want to come back to the city for a while. Just because things have, well, changed, there's no reason that we can't all try and get along . . .

Ollie. I don't want to come in right now. I've been busy, actually. She had gone to a lecture at Guild Hall, to movie night at the library, and to half of a yoga class (which she still hated). It wasn't much, but it was more social interaction than she usually had in three months. She needed to get her mind off Maze.

Even though she knew Ollie thought she was bullshitting him, that she was really spending her time reading and napping like she normally did, he tried a new tactic to get her to come to the city.

Well, that's great. But Clem would love to see you.

Clem. Oliver said it like it was true. Like Clem hadn't given up, was still waiting for her.

Put her on the phone.

Now?

Of course now.

She's in her room.

Well, get her.

Hang on. She heard Ollie walk up the stairs with the phone. Then he put it on hold.

Um, Althea . . . it's a bad time, he said when he came back on.

She doesn't want to talk to me.

It's not that.

Yes, it is.

Well, maybe. You could try again later.

No, Ollie. I know Clem. She won't ever talk to me. Tell her she doesn't have to talk. Just listen.

I'll see what she says.

Okay. After a minute, Clem got on.

What is it?

How are you?

This sounds like a conversation to me. I'm hanging up.

Please. I just wanted to say I'm sorry.

Silence.

Did you hear me?

Silence.

I'm sorry for being such a terrible mom. For not trying. Or for not even knowing how to try.

Silence.

Maybe you should have gone to another family. Had another mother. I don't know. But your dad always loved you. You always have that. I just . . .

Lune . . . at least you are done pretending. It wasn't like I couldn't tell. The brown sea glass — that's you, you know. You just make the green ones look even better.

Althea thought of Clem throwing the pieces of brown sea glass back into the ocean. Keeping a few not out of hope but because of how ugly they were. To remind herself what a shitty mother she had.

Now she was done talking. What could Althea say? Thanks for your honesty? See you around?

Well, Clem, you have Claire now. That should make you happy.

I guess.

Why do you guess?

You don't get it. I'm not looking for anyone anymore. I wanted you.

Althea could hear the trace of a question in Clem's voice: Lune, could you possibly have wanted me too? Just a tiny bit? Or maybe you could now? Althea held her breath. Maybe she could lie. Tell Clem that yes, she had wanted things to be different. Even that would be better than nothing. How hard would saying that be? But it just wasn't true. Maybe she had come to like Clem, but she knew she would never love her. And that Clem would get over it. Just like Althea was starting to with Maze. Or, not really, but she knew in time she would.

Clem, give Claire a chance. You'll see.

If that's what you want.

She knew that replying, It is, would be too cruel.

Instead:

Not exactly, but —

Clem interrupted. *I get it, Lune. Just please stop talking now. You're only making it worse and I don't want to hear it.* And she hung up the phone. Clem, the ten-year-old whom she called her daughter, hung up on her.

Althea expected to feel relief, but she didn't, really. What did she have now? She had given away her family. Maze had not exactly given her away, but he had left. She had no plans for the present moment. Didn't know what she was going to do or even where she was going to live in the fall. She wasn't sad so much as bewildered. But she was okay. She was alone, but she was okay.

ACKNOWLEDGMENTS

My three chickens, who maybe someday will read this book: Alexander, Vanessa, and Camilla.

My amazing mother, Abra Wilkin, who gets me more than anyone.

My wonderful siblings, who comment only when necessary: Abra Williams and Anthony Anderson.

My dear "step-ins": Jim Wilkin, Pamela Sherrod Anderson, Betsy and Buzz Norton.

The generous adults who took an interest in me when I was a child and who have stuck with me since: Ron and Christina Gidwitz, David Weber.

Lola Vautrin, Betty Wang, Rick Fiscina, Jane Power, Carrie Karasysov. The word *friends* doesn't begin to cover it.

Laura Duane, Ashley Burke, Katie Nicolas, Lindsay Bliven. A room of one's own doesn't cut it these days; a woman needs childcare.

Bill Clegg, Adrienne Brodeur, Lauren Wein, Tracy Roe. For joining my party of one in taking my work seriously. I could cry.

Dave Matthews, Chris Martin. No explanation needed.